Following the success of Project: Notice Me, Kyle and Aidan are now in a three-month extension of their play. If three months wasn't so short, then it would be everything Kyle wants.

They've been together long enough to meet each other's friends and to try new things. Kyle only hopes that at the end of the three months, he isn't the only one who wants more.

TO HAVE AND TO HOLD

Enchanting Encounters, Book Two

Tamryn Eradani

A NineStar Press Publication

Published by NineStar Press
P.O. Box 91792,
Albuquerque, New Mexico, 87199 USA.
www.ninestarpress.com

To Have and to Hold

Printed in the USA
First Edition
June, 2018

Print ISBN: 978-1-948608-92-3

Also available in eBook, ISBN: 978-1-948608-82-4

Warning: This book contains sexually explicit content, which may only be suitable for mature readers.

Chapter One

"I CAN DRIVE myself tonight," Kyle says as he rummages through his closet for the third time in the past five minutes. Jenny's been here for fifteen, amused as he worked himself into a panic, but now her arms are crossed over her chest, and she's moving into impatient territory as he can't settle on what he wants to wear. "You and Charlotte should head out."

Tonight, Kyle's two best friends, Jenny and Charlotte, are meeting his Dom for the first time.

Kyle's been crushing on Aidan since the first time he saw him at Enchanting Encounters, the kink club he's been frequenting for years now. After he managed to catch Aidan's attention, they had a two-week trial period to see if they were compatible beyond physical attraction.

Now that they've extended their play to a three-month commitment, Kyle figures it's time Aidan met the most important people in his life.

Well, that, and Jenny was determined to meet Aidan, whether Kyle was there or not, and he doesn't need Jenny scaring him off.

"We're not leaving you behind," Jenny says. She sprawls across Kyle's bed, making herself comfortable.

"Absolutely not," Charlotte agrees, wandering in. She lies down next to Jenny, resting her head on Jenny's stomach. "I'm not sure you'd ever make it."

"Besides, if you drive in with me and Charlotte and we have to leave early, then you'll have no choice but to catch a ride home with your man."

"Huh," Kyle says. It's a good point. It's a Wednesday night which means Aidan has afternoon classes tomorrow. Maybe he could go home with Aidan. Or have Aidan come home with him. As long as there's bed sharing involved, Kyle isn't picky on whose bed they sleep in.

"Never say I don't do anything for you," Jenny tells him. Then, "Put down that shirt. It's basically see-through."

"It looks good on me," Kyle points out, but he puts the shirt back because it's not appropriate for where they're going. He picks up one of his polos and glances at his small collection of dress shirts. "Is this a date?"

"Ugh," Jenny groans.

"Would it be bad if it was?" Charlotte asks.

"You've already seen each other naked," Jenny says. "This can't be more intimidating than that."

"We haven't actually seen each other naked," Kyle says. That is something he's going to change as soon as possible. "And you're trying to distract me. Scenes are scenes and dates are dates. They're different."

"Put a damn shirt on so we can go," Jenny says.

Kyle grabs a long-sleeve thermal to throw on. Shirt and jeans on, he only has one thing left to do. "Overnight bag."

"I take it back," Jenny says. "You can drive yourself, and every minute you're late is a minute I have to ask Aidan questions."

"Nope, you said you were giving me a ride. No takebacks."

Packing an overnight bag is quicker than dressing himself for this maybe-date. Socks, boxers, pajamas, a black V-neck, his favorite briefs, and a toothbrush. He already has condoms and lube stashed in his bag, and he can't think of anything else he might need.

"All set," Kyle says.

"Fucking finally."

"On second thought." Kyle runs a hand through his hair. "Maybe…"

"No," Jenny says. She jumps out of bed so she can slam Kyle's bathroom door shut, cutting him off from his comb and his hair gel, and Kyle dissolves into laughter.

"All right," Charlotte says, but she smiles at both of them. "Let's go. We don't want to be late. I want to make a good impression on Aidan."

"He'll love you," Kyle promises.

Charlotte pats his cheek. "Then there's nothing for you to worry about."

Except I want him to love me *too.*

Kyle links his arm through Charlotte's. "Come on, I'm in the mood for a beer and pretzels dipped in cheese sauce."

"Gross," Jenny says and leads them out the door.

THE BAR THEY go to is the one Kyle visits when he wants to yell at his basketball team with other disgruntled fans or when he wants a drink without worrying about hooking up. It's fairly crowded tonight, because Wednesday nights boast twenty-five cent wings. The only place for the four of them to sit without having to wait is at the bar.

Kyle drops his jacket on their fourth barstool so no one will take Aidan's seat before he gets there.

He pulls the bowl of popcorn on the counter closer to him and sifts through it until he finds a particularly buttered piece. He's chewing when a hand settles on his shoulder. He smiles even before he turns and confirms that it's Aidan.

"Hey," Kyle says.

Aidan squeezes Kyle's shoulder and says, "Good evening," because he always uses more words than he needs to say things. Kyle thinks it's a byproduct of being a college professor. Or maybe that's why he became a professor, so he'd have an excuse to talk all the time.

Hand still on Kyle's shoulder, Aidan reaches his other hand out to Jenny. "I'm Aidan," he says as if Jenny hasn't done almost as much research on him as Kyle has.

"Jenny." She shakes his hand.

Next to her, Charlotte waves. "I'm Charlotte. Nice to meet you."

"Likewise."

Likewise, Kyle mouths because who even says that? Charlotte covers her grin with her hand.

"I hope I didn't keep you from ordering." Aidan picks Kyle's jacket up so he can pull his stool closer to Kyle before he sits down. Their knees touch now, Kyle's jeans against Aidan's khakis, and Kyle leans into his side.

"We just got here," Charlotte assures him.

"I don't care what you order as long as there are mozzarella sticks and I can have at least four," Jenny says.

Kyle turns to Aidan and whispers, loudly enough for Jenny to hear, "She's terrible at sharing."

Aidan laughs and drops his hand to Kyle's knee. "I have no feelings on mozzarella sticks, but I prefer my buffalo chicken to be boneless."

"That takes all the fun out of it," Kyle says. "Which, I suppose, is why you like them that way." He laughs as Aidan pinches him and swats him with the menu. "We could just skip the bickering and eat popcorn with our drinks."

"No," Jenny says, pointing at him. "We swore after college we would never do that again."

"We got trashed," Kyle explains for Aidan's benefit, "and we decided we were too drunk to find food or even call out for pizza so we'd do something easy. I think we made ten bags of popcorn."

"And ate all of them," Jenny finishes. "Not one of our finer moments."

"No," Kyle agrees.

"How about the sampler?" Charlotte asks, menu open in front of her. "It comes with mozzarella sticks, buffalo chicken tenders, regular chicken tenders, and onion rings."

"But only three mozzarella sticks," Jenny pouts.

"And you love the spring rolls here," Kyle says.

"I would split spring rolls with you," Aidan tells Charlotte.

"It's decided." Kyle closes his menu. "The sampler and an order of spring rolls." He rolls his eyes at Jenny. "You can have all the mozzarella sticks."

"But there's only three."

They order their appetizers and their drinks when the bartender swings by, and it isn't long before Kyle has a rum and Coke with an umbrella sticking out of it.

"You're a child," Jenny tells him.

"Umbrellas automatically make any drink cooler." Kyle eyes Aidan's beer like he wants to stick his umbrella in it, and Aidan pulls his bottle to safety. Kyle huffs. "Why do I hang out with boring people?"

"I knew I should've worn my *Pete the Cat* sweater tonight," Charlotte says.

"She's a children's librarian," Kyle tells Aidan, "and has outfits for basically every major series. Wait until you see her *Charlotte's Web* getup."

"It's funny because my name is Charlotte," she explains.

Aidan grins and takes a sip of his beer.

"If we're talking poor fashion choices then I should break out the pictures from Kyle's fishnet phase," Jenny says.

"Are you saying you don't like my work-appropriate sweaters?" Charlotte asks.

"Uh," Jenny says.

"I was a teenager," Kyle tells Aidan. "Lestat was a formative influence on me."

"The fishnet and mesh shirts stuck around for a while," Jenny says, her arm draped over Charlotte's shoulder now. "Thankfully, your attempts at singing did not."

"I have a beautiful voice," Kyle says. "We should've gone somewhere with karaoke."

"No," Jenny and Charlotte say at the same time, forceful enough that Kyle's feelings are a little hurt.

Aidan pats Kyle's thigh, a reminder that Kyle has one person here who's guaranteed to be on his side.

He still takes a sulky sip of his drink.

His real revenge, though, comes when he swipes a mozzarella stick from their sampler. He takes an obnoxious bite and grins at Jenny while he chews.

"You don't even like mozzarella sticks."

"Worth it," he says before handing the half-eaten appetizer to Aidan. "Here, I don't like these."

Aidan bursts out laughing.

"No, don't encourage him."

"Too late," Kyle says, smirking as he leans back against Aidan's chest. "He likes me just the way I am."

LATER, ONCE THEY'VE finished their food and are mostly done with their second drinks, Jenny and Charlotte go to the bathroom together.

"Lucky guys," a man passing by them says. He nods toward the little hallway Jenny and Charlotte disappeared down.

Kyle looks at the man. His business suit is wrinkled at the elbows and behind the knees. He sounds completely sincere as if he doesn't notice how Kyle's pressed up against Aidan's side or how Charlotte and Jenny held hands as they navigated the crowded bar.

"Yeah," Kyle says. "We're real lucky."

The man in the suit nods as if he's done something good and wanders away.

"Does this happen a lot?" Aidan asks.

"A fair amount. We usually have a couple laughs about it later. But if the assumptions bother you, then I can kiss you."

Aidan's eyes crinkle at the corners when he smiles. "Maybe I'll take you up on that offer later."

In private, because exhibitionism isn't a thing for him the way it is for me.

"Speaking of, Jenny gave me a ride here, if you want to drive me home. To either of our homes."

"More of your clever planning?" Aidan asks, teasing.

He never should've told Aidan about his plan to get his attention through a series of public scenes at Enchanting Encounters. It's opened him up to being teased for the rest of his life. Though, since his plan *worked*, he doesn't mind the teasing too much.

"Jenny's idea, actually." Because he knows he's pushy sometimes, he adds, "I can catch a ride back with them. Or you can drop me off. I know we didn't have anything planned."

"Do you want to do something?"

"Sleep in a bed with you," Kyle answers which isn't the sexy or fun answer but is the honest one. "I wouldn't say no to anything else, but I know you have work tomorrow."

"Work in the afternoon." Aidan pulls Kyle closer to him and Kyle rests his head on Aidan's shoulder. "We could talk about something tonight and do it tomorrow morning. Or we could just sleep."

Kyle hasn't known Aidan long enough to read him and know what Aidan would rather do. Kyle would be happy with either, but he'd be happiest with what Aidan wants. He knows better than to say that, though. Aidan's last sub, Simon, did a real number on his head. The kid had been new to the scene and wanted Aidan to like him so badly he agreed to things he didn't want because he thought it would make Aidan keep him.

It means Kyle has to be careful he doesn't dip too far into that territory. Most of the time, it isn't a problem. Kyle usually has clear ideas of what he wants and when he wants it, but tonight, he doesn't want to make the decision.

If he's being honest with himself, he doesn't want to push for too much.

He knows exactly what he wants; Aidan in his bed so tomorrow morning he can make him breakfast and maybe exchange some lazy kisses in the shower before he sends Aidan off to work, but that seems like it's moving too fast.

But if Aidan offers it...

No.

He won't be a coward.

He turns so he and Aidan are facing each other. "Yes, on sleeping together. We can talk out the rest of it when we're home. Your place or mine?" He summons his sleaziest grin in an effort to tempt a smile back onto Aidan's face.

Aidan smiles and shakes his head, aiming for disapproving but landing closer to fond. "Yours? That way, I can leave for work without worrying about how to get you back to your place."

"Plus, I have real food in my fridge."

"You're cooking for me?"

"One of the many services I have to offer."

Kyle smiles and leans in, hoping for a kiss, but they're interrupted by Jenny's, "Ugh," as she drops into her seat. "We came back at the wrong time."

Kyle rolls his eyes. "We're talking about breakfast. Relax."

"So you don't need a ride home, then?" Charlotte asks.

Kyle has a joke about riding on the tip of his tongue, but Aidan says, "We're all set but thank you," before he can make it.

"We should do this again," Charlotte says. "It was fun."

"Game night?" Kyle asks. "Wine and Scrabble? We haven't done that in a while."

"Mr. Professor over there might have an advantage," Jenny says.

Kyle rolls his eyes. "Charlotte's a librarian. The game might actually be interesting for once."

"Hey!" Jenny protests.

Kyle grins as he tells Aidan, "I like to make tiny words that block off the board."

"Why am I not surprised?"

Kyle pulls his wallet out, pleased to see his friends get along. He tosses a couple of bills on the counter and waves Aidan off when he reaches for his wallet. "I covered our half." He can't keep the smile off his face, and Jenny groans.

"This might be worse than the pining."

He cheerfully flips her off. "We're going now. I'll text you about lunch tomorrow."

Kyle slides off his stool and kisses Charlotte's cheek and hugs Jenny before he follows Aidan out of the bar. In the parking lot, he wraps Aidan's arm around his waist.

"This okay?" Kyle asks.

Aidan tugs him closer and hooks his thumb through Kyle's belt loop. "It is now."

Kyle's tempted to stop in the middle of the parking lot and kiss him, but he knows better than to start something he won't be able to finish. It'll be more fun to wait until they're in Kyle's apartment where Kyle can kiss Aidan for the first time against his door and against his island counter and on his couch and in his *bed*.

Kyle grins and quickens his step.

It's a short drive to Kyle's apartment, and Kyle directs Aidan to the empty spaces in front of Building 3, and maybe he directs Aidan to park next to his car. It makes something flutter in his chest to see their cars side by side, and he's glad the dark hides the goofy smile on his face.

They don't touch on their way to Kyle's apartment, and Kyle's not sure if it's Aidan's dislike of public displays of affection or something different, but he follows Aidan's lead and keeps his distance until they're inside the apartment.

Once the door closes, though, Kyle pushes into Aidan's space, demanding to make up for lost time.

Aidan's overnight bag thuds softly as it hits the ground, straps slipping out of Aidan's fingers as soon as Kyle pushes him up against the door. *First location checked off the list*, Kyle thinks as he kisses Aidan with enough force to catch him off guard. It doesn't take long for Aidan to catch up, wrapping an arm around Kyle's waist to pull him closer.

It's an encouragement, and it makes Kyle bold enough to push for more. He takes every inch he's given and slides his thigh between Aidan's to take more. He grinds his thigh against Aidan's cock, half-hard and growing harder, and Kyle groans into the kiss. The only way they could be closer would be if they lost their clothes and...well, that's not a bad idea.

Kyle keeps one hand tucked into the back pocket of Aidan's pants. The other is at the hem of Aidan's shirt, trying to shove it up and off. He doesn't get far before Aidan spins them so it's Kyle with his back against the door.

It isn't a bad position, trapped between the solid wood of the door and the solid press of Aidan's body but then Aidan pins Kyle's hands against the door, and he can't help his whine. He pulls against Aidan's grip, half because he wants Aidan to hold him down harder and half because he wants to break free.

"I want to touch you," Kyle says, turning his mouth away from Aidan's. "Please, I'll make it so good." He flexes his fingers, straining for something he's not allowed to have. He kisses Aidan's neck, careful not to suck too hard or use his teeth because Aidan has to stand in front of a classroom of college students tomorrow. "Let me? Please?"

There are so many places he could touch if his hands were allowed to roam beneath Aidan's shirt. And if Aidan took his shirt off, then Kyle could leave all the marks he wants. Red lines from Kyle's nails down Aidan's back and little bite marks above the cut of his hips.

Kyle wants Aidan splayed across his bed, hair sex-mussed, lips swollen from being kissed, and a myriad of marks left by Kyle's nails and teeth covering his body. He wants Aidan exhausted and pleased and to hold his arms open for Kyle to join him.

He kisses the underside of Aidan's jaw, and it's a struggle to keep from digging his teeth into the skin there, from leaving a mark which says *he's mine, back off.*

"Please," Kyle says again and when he closes his eyes his lashes sweep against Aidan's skin.

Aidan lifts Kyle's hands off the door, and Kyle feels a surge of victory before Aidan places them on his torso instead.

Above his shirt.

At least Kyle can feel the tremble of Aidan's body beneath his hands, the only sign that Aidan's even as close to affected as Kyle is.

"You can have what I offer you," Aidan says. "Nothing more."

"Seriously?" Kyle asks, sliding his hands over the fabric of Aidan's shirt. "Are you sure this isn't a thing?"

In all the time they've been together—admittedly, it's not very much—they've never been completely naked together. Kyle wants to see and touch and *taste*. He wants Aidan stripped for him so he can try to soak in his fill.

Kyle's been fucked by Aidan, and he's blown him, but he's never seen Aidan's dick. He's never even seen the man shirtless, and at this rate, Kyle's afraid these next three months will be more of the same.

"The clothes?" Aidan asks with a grin. "Or denying you things you want to watch you work yourself up over them?" He trails a finger down the slope of Kyle's jaw. "Because that's definitely a thing."

Kyle groans and slumps against the door. *So much for a quiet night at home.*

Aidan laughs, his breath hot against Kyle's cheek. "I thought you wanted to touch me." There's a challenge in his words.

"I do." But he knows himself, knows he could easily get lost in touching and kissing and lose track of time. "But I was also promised a bed." He nudges Aidan's bag with his foot. "Pajamas and then we can pick things up where we left off?"

"Sounds good." Aidan drops a light kiss on Kyle's mouth before he takes a step back. "And we should talk about this more. We also promised a discussion when we arrived."

"Oops." Kyle runs a hand through his hair. "Do you want the bathroom first? Or do you want me to close my eyes until you tell me you're dressed?"

"Hilarious," Aidan says.

Kyle grins. "One of my many charms. Come on, I'll give you the brief tour of the apartment and then we can get back to kissing. Question, though, the clothes thing. Can *I* sleep shirtless or does your Victorian kink go both ways?"

"Brat," Aidan says, and Kyle laughs and grabs his hand to lead him into the kitchen.

Chapter Two

KYLE'S THE FIRST one awake in the morning, and he doesn't know Aidan well enough yet to know if this is something he should expect. Maybe, in a few weeks, he'll know if Aidan's the kind of person who sleeps in whenever he has the chance or if he's groggy when he wakes up to his alarm or if he's the kind of person who likes to sleep with the curtains open so he wakes up with the sun.

There are dozens of little things they don't know about each other, and Kyle wants to learn them all.

But for now he eases out of bed and tucks Aidan's arm around a pillow. Aidan makes a low grumbling sound as he pulls the pillow closer. It's as if even while asleep he knows he's being tricked.

"I'll be right back," Kyle murmurs before going to the bathroom to take a piss and brush his teeth.

When he emerges from the bathroom, Aidan is still asleep, turned on his side and curled around the pillow. A quick glance at the clock tells Kyle he has ten minutes before he's even allowed to think about waking Aidan up.

They talked about this last night, what they each wanted out of this morning, and it took some negotiating, but Kyle thinks they've come up with a scene they'll both enjoy. Aidan doesn't seem sold on why Kyle wants what he wants so badly, but Kyle hopes to show him.

He sits on the edge of the bed so he can put his cuffs on. They're black leather and padded, and they're easy enough to buckle himself, but he prefers to have his Dom do it for him.

This morning, he does it himself because it's what he and Aidan agreed on last night. He can't help but feel cheated, though, that their first scene with his cuffs is one where he puts them on himself. Maybe next time, Kyle can hold his wrists out to Aidan and watch as Aidan buckles them into place.

The leather looks good against his skin, not as good as brown would, but he likes the contrast of the black against the silver of the buckles and the rings. These are well-made, sturdy, and he rotates his wrists as he admires them.

When he and Aidan agreed to their three-month exclusive partnership, they decided on using Kyle's cuffs as a sign they're in a scene. For their two-week trial period, they stayed in the club, and there it was easy to know when they were in-scene and when they were out of it. Now that they'll be using each other's homes, it's good to have a visual and verbal cue.

Some people use collars for that, but where Kyle's concerned, a collar is for more than play. It has meaning behind it, and he rarely scenes with one, because to him they're a sign of a committed partnership. He doesn't want to wear one unless he's with someone who deserves it.

Maybe...

Kyle shakes his head. He's been with Aidan for two weeks, and if things go well, then they'll have another three months together. It's certainly a start, but it won't do Kyle any good to get too far ahead of himself.

He checks the clock again.

It's time.

He wants to brush his fingers against Aidan's cheek, pink from all the blankets he has pulled over him, or maybe run his hands through Aidan's hair, light brown and pressed flat against his pillow.

Instead, he eases his drawer open and pulls out a condom then tips Aidan onto his back. Tugging the blankets down without waking him up is more difficult, but once they're at the foot of the bed, Aidan's legs part, as if, even in his sleep, he knows what's about to happen.

He only pulls Aidan's pajama pants down far enough to lift his cock out, soft after a long night of sleep, and warm from where it's been nestled in Aidan's pants. Kyle's been fucked by Aidan, and he's even had his cock in his mouth, but he was fucked from behind, and the last time he blew Aidan he was blindfolded.

This is Kyle's first time seeing it, the head a blushing pink, the same color as Aidan's lips. Kyle wants to linger, to touch and stare his fill, but he knows he only has a small window before Aidan wakes up.

There's something vulnerable about seeing him soft. He wants to press a featherlight kiss to the tip, but he settles for rubbing his cheek against the sleep-warm skin instead. Aidan's cock firms up enough for Kyle to roll the condom on, gentle, so he doesn't bring Aidan out of his sleep.

He props himself up on his elbows to stare then pushes Aidan's shirt up enough to lay a kiss just below his belly button, and Aidan's stomach tightens, and he breathes out a small sigh as his fingers lose their grip on his pillow. Kyle eases the pillow out of Aidan's grasp and redirects Aidan's hands to his hair instead.

They curl there, but don't pull tight the way they might if he was awake.

Kyle bends his head again so he can take Aidan in his mouth. Early in the morning, with Aidan asleep and Kyle still not completely awake, there's no rush here. Kyle can close his eyes and focus on the way Aidan grows hard in his mouth.

Aidan's hard for *him*, from the wet heat of Kyle's mouth and the way his tongue flutters against Aidan's length. With his eyes closed and the room quiet, there's nothing to distract Kyle from the heavy weight of Aidan's cock.

Usually when Kyle blows someone, it's with purpose. He wants to see them lose their control or maybe he wants to tempt them into fucking him. There's something unhurried right now that makes him wish he could be patient like this more often.

He takes Aidan as deep as he can from this angle. Once he's full of Aidan's cock, just this side of too much, he lays his hands on Aidan's stomach so when he opens his eyes the first thing he'll see is his cuffs, the black leather standing out against the white of Aidan's sleep shirt.

Like this, he's surrounded by Aidan—the feel of him in his mouth, the musky scent of sex and lighter scent of sleep mingling and putting Kyle even more at ease. He doesn't think he could fall asleep like this, but his body and his head are so settled he thinks he could drift for hours.

This is a headspace he usually struggles to reach, but Aidan's managed to put him here without even being awake for it.

He casts his gaze up, grateful and longing for Aidan to be awake to experience this with him, only to find Aidan staring back at him. Immediately, Kyle tightens up, afraid of everything he might be broadcasting in his eyes, but Aidan pets his hair, gentle and reassuring.

"This is a pleasant way to wake up." Aidan pushes Kyle's hair away from his forehead. "Thank you."

Aidan brushes his thumb across Kyle's heated cheek the same way Kyle wanted to do to him this morning. It makes him want to touch Aidan again, makes him greedy for more than he's been given, and he curls his fingers against Aidan's shirt.

The movement's enough to draw Aidan's gaze to Kyle's cuffs, and he lifts Kyle's right wrist in careful hands. His fingers touch and explore the cuff and the strap, the buckle and the rings. He even slips a finger beneath the leather to check the padding. It's sweet and maybe unnecessary, but he does the same with Kyle's left wrist, until Kyle's trembling in his hold.

"They're nice," Aidan says.

They're Kyle's first real cuffs, and he's used them at the club to hold his wrists together above his head and show off the long line of his body. He's clipped them together behind his back to show his body off in other ways. He's let Doms curl their fingers through the rings to tug him around. He's worn them in his apartment while he jerked himself off, because he likes the look of leather against his wrists.

He wants new memories to add to these ones. He wants to see what memories Aidan will press into the leather for Kyle to conjure when he's alone in his room.

Aidan cards his fingers through Kyle's hair, his fingertips rubbing little circles against Kyle's scalp. Kyle wants to tip his head into the touch like a cat demanding to be pet, but he doesn't want to move so he hums instead, hoping to convey that he doesn't want Aidan to stop touching him.

Aidan jerks his hips up as if he'd forgotten Kyle has his cock in his mouth, and Kyle has to pull off, coughing and wiping his mouth.

"Sorry," Aidan says.

"It's okay. If that's what you want—" Kyle doesn't get any further before Aidan shakes his head.

"Not right now. This is good. You, uh—" Aidan curls his fingers under Kyle's chin. "You really like this."

Kyle smiles, both at the wonder in Aidan's voice and the surprise. "I asked for it last night." He glances down at Aidan's dick, hard now and curving up toward his stomach. "Can I?"

Aidan nods and Kyle dips his head back down. He smiles when Aidan's hands pet his hair again. And Aidan rolls his hips, a slow, sinuous movement that Kyle's prepared for, and he doesn't choke this time.

He closes his eyes and gives himself over to the feel of Aidan's hands in his hair and the drag of his cock, and the words Aidan murmurs, full of wonder and praise. When Kyle told Aidan he wanted to wake him up by blowing him, this honestly isn't the direction Kyle thought it would go in.

He expected it to be a tease, something to wind them both up until Aidan flipped them and took the pleasure Kyle was offering. This is...not necessarily better, but Kyle enjoys it more than he thought he would.

He likes the way Aidan touches him, careful, not because Kyle's fragile but because he's precious. He likes the way Aidan watches him, reverent and openly appreciative. He really likes knowing he's the one to put that look on Aidan's face and that gentleness in his hands.

He feels *good*.

He casts his gaze up. Aidan smiles down at him and warmth and satisfaction fill Kyle's chest. He could float like this for hours, he thinks, as long as Aidan continued to touch him and talk to him like this.

When Aidan finally comes, it's with his thumbs sweeping across Kyle's cheekbones. He keeps Aidan's cock in his mouth until he slumps back against the bed. Then Kyle pulls off, careful because he knows Aidan's sensitive.

Aidan removes the condom and ties it off as Kyle works his jaw. It's a little sore, but mostly it feels empty, and Kyle wrinkles his nose at the feeling. He...he felt so good only seconds ago and now he's not quite right, like a painting knocked crooked from where it hangs.

"Come here," Aidan says, and Kyle moves up Aidan's body until Aidan can pull him down for a kiss.

It helps settle him enough that he's the first to break the kiss. "Shower?" Kyle asks. "Fifteen minutes good? Twenty maybe if I get dressed before I make us breakfast. There are spare towels in the closet. Eggs and French toast okay?"

"Are you trying to spoil me?"

Kyle grins and leans in for another kiss, which is both a not-answer and a complete answer all at once. He's halfway out of bed when Aidan hooks his fingers through the ring on his left cuff. Kyle instantly stills and looks to Aidan, wondering if Aidan knows how many times Kyle's imagined him doing that just this morning alone.

"What do you want?" Aidan asks.

"To make you breakfast."

Aidan smiles as if he thinks Kyle didn't understand him and dips his first two fingers into Kyle's waistband.

Kyle smiles back. "Really, I want to make you breakfast."

"But you—we—"

Aidan looks confused enough that Kyle takes pity on him. "It's not an exchange. I mean, it is, that is literally what we do, but —" Kyle glances down at his wrist, at Aidan's fingers still hooked through the ring there as he gathers his thoughts into something more coherent. "I wanted to blow you, you wanted me to blow you, we both got what we wanted. That really did it for me. Not in a sex way, in a different way. I'm not saying I never want to come again, but like —" Kyle makes a face. "Talking is fucking overrated."

Aidan huffs out a laugh and reels Kyle back in to kiss the frown off his face. "If you're happy, then I believe you. I don't need to understand."

"But you want to."

Aidan curls his other hand around Kyle's hip and brings him closer again. "The way you looked—completely at peace, *happy*, yes, I want to understand. I want to know how exactly to put that look on your face again and again."

"Oh," Kyle says. "Let's start with breakfast. I want to do that for you. Will you let me?"

"Yes," Aidan answers, but he pulls Kyle in for another lingering kiss before he finally lets him go.

Kyle keeps his ears trained for any noise as he moves into the kitchen, which is how he knows it takes Aidan almost five full minutes to turn the shower on after Kyle leaves him in the bedroom. Pride blooms in his chest, because he did that. He wanted to start Aidan's morning out right, and so far, he has.

Aidan's shower goes long, but Kyle eats the first batch of eggs and the first few slices of French toast which means the second batch is just finishing up when Aidan emerges from the bathroom with damp hair and his pajamas back on.

He pauses when he sees the stack of French toast and the plate of eggs on the table. Kyle set them up at the breakfast nook, because the island counter is too tall for what he wants.

"There's only one plate," Aidan says as he sits down.

"I ate while I was cooking. I wanted..." Kyle folds to his knees between Aidan's legs and rests his head on Aidan's thigh. "Is this okay?"

Aidan ruffles his hair. "It's good."

He leaves his hand in Kyle's hair as he eats and tells him how good breakfast is in between his plans for his day, and by the time Aidan leaves for work, Kyle's buzzing and feeling like he can take on the world.

Once Aidan's gone, Kyle sits in front of his laptop, and he only rubs his bare wrists together once before he pulls up his list of current projects. He's sent three to clients for review and is working through the fourth when Jenny shows up for lunch.

"Wow," Jenny says when she sees him.

There aren't any marks on him anywhere, no sign that Aidan was here, no hint of what they did last night or this morning so Kyle doesn't know what she sees, but he can't help his answering smile. "Yeah."

"Good night?"

"Night was okay. This morning was better."

Jenny laughs and plucks his laptop from him so she can look through his work while he makes lunch. "I'm glad things are working out for you two."

The mention of working out reminds Kyle he should make it down to the gym at some point tonight. He takes pride in his body, both what it can do and what it looks like. Jenny calls him vain, but that's not quite right. Or maybe it is, but he doesn't think there's anything wrong with his eyes lingering on himself in the mirror or in wanting other people to stare at him.

And now that he's Aidan's for the next three months, he wants Aidan to take pride in his body too. He wants to be someone for Aidan to show off.

"What'd you think of him?" Kyle asks as he puts the chicken in the oven.

"These are pretty good," Jenny says, ignoring Kyle's question as she points to his laptop screen. "Whatever you did this morning, you should do it more often."

"That's the plan." Kyle sets the timer on the oven and leans against the counter as he waits for his water to boil. "So? Meeting one was good? We can plan our Scrabble night?"

Jenny closes Kyle's laptop screen. "Do you think you're moving out of the club too fast?"

"Seriously?" Kyle asks. He doesn't want Jenny's *worry*, he wants her approval.

"You've known him for two weeks."

"We didn't do anything intense or potentially dangerous," Kyle says. "We're—I'm not stupid. And contrary to popular belief, I do know how to look after myself."

"That's not what I meant. You just—you really like him."

"Yes, I like him. Yes, I pursued him. No, I'm not going to be stupid now that I have him."

"I'm sorry," Jenny says. "I didn't mean to imply you don't know how to watch out for yourself. I just don't want you to get hurt. He seems nice. And like you'll walk all over him."

She offers Kyle a smile, and Kyle smiles back, because he can never stay angry at Jenny for long, especially when she's trying to be a good friend.

"So far, that hasn't been the case," Kyle says. "I can give you details if you want."

"I most certainly don't want," Jenny says with a laugh. "All I need to know is if you're happy and if you're safe."

"I definitely am." Kyle fishes the asparagus out of the fridge. "We should set up a time for the photoshoot I owe you."

"Oh? I figured we weren't on for that anymore."

"I made you a promise."

"Aidan's okay with it? He seems territorial, and you two are pretty new. I'm a Dom he doesn't know and—"

"You're my friend," Kyle says. "And if he can't respect me having friends or talking to other Doms, then we won't last. You're not a threat to what he and I have. If he doesn't know that yet, then I'll make sure to show him."

"Okay," Jenny says. "What about demos at the club?"

"I thought you didn't want details."

Jenny holds her hands up. "All right, one last question. Does Aidan want to be at the shoot? He can be as long as he isn't in my way, but I reserve the right to kick him out."

"He doesn't want to be there, but I'll see him after. We haven't quite worked out the details yet." Kyle grins.

"I don't want them," Jenny reminds him. She holds her arms open. "Hug? And then I'm going to complain about work until you feed me."

Kyle laughs and puts the asparagus in the pan.

AFTER LUNCH, KYLE works for another hour before he heads down to the gym, which doubles as both a workout and a break, because he watches TV while he's on the treadmill. A quick shower, a snack, and two more hours of work later, his phone rings.

"Hey," Kyle says, smiling as he answers Aidan's call. "How were your classes?"

"The first one was good. The second was missing several students, because they had a paper due and they seem to think that if they're not in class, then I won't penalize them for not turning it in."

Kyle had taken mostly art classes, which meant projects had a midnight due date and most of the time class was used to work on their projects. On the rare occasions he did have to write papers, he'd spend hours in the library, hours knocking his head against his desk. So, yeah, he can sympathize with Aidan's students.

"I have fifteen minutes before my third class," Aidan continues, "but I wanted to talk to you."

Kyle grins stupidly at his phone.

"How's your afternoon been?"

"Productive. I did a bunch of work, went to the gym, made a kickass lunch."

"I take it from your enthusiasm that this isn't the normal course of a day for you."

Kyle laughs. "Not quite. There are some days I have to turn the internet off if I want to get anything done, but today was good. I was focused, I was efficient. I must've started my day off right."

"French toast and eggs is a good combination of carbohydrates and protein."

Kyle laughs again, something warm and bubbly rising in his chest. "Yeah, that must've been it. You said you have fifteen minutes?"

"Closer to five now," Aidan says. "I shouldn't be on my phone when my students come in. They might begin to think of me as human."

"I'd hate to ruin your image even if I think you're lying. You're probably one of the cool professors."

"Definitely not," Aidan says, and Kyle can hear the embarrassment in his voice. And maybe even a little pleasure? "I certainly don't think so."

"Uh-huh. Well, I won't hold you too long. Can I call you later tonight?"

"Of course. You can call me anytime. If it's an emergency send me a text, and I'll dismiss my class early and pick up."

"No, not—" Kyle smiles helplessly at his phone again. "That's not what I meant, but good to know. Thank you."

"You don't need to thank me for doing the right thing."

"Noted. But back to my original question. Can I call you tonight and maybe you don't answer?"

There's a beat of silence before Aidan says, "Ah. Yeah, you can do that. Send me a text first, so I know I shouldn't pick up."

"Maybe after your phone call, I can call you again and you pick up and we can talk about this weekend."

"Definitely." He's tempted to tease, but Aidan has to be in class in five minutes and Kyle isn't cruel. He'll have plenty of time later to have fun. "I'm headed into the club tomorrow to talk to Wanda, so I'll book us a room while I'm there."

"Sounds good. I'll talk to you tonight."

Kyle makes a kissing sound at his phone and hangs up.

Chapter Three

AFTER SUCH A productive day, Kyle rewards himself with a complicated dinner. He pulls HGTV up on his computer for background noise as he moves around his kitchen, losing himself in the comfort of chopping and slicing and cooking. After dinner, he settles in front of the couch with a glass of wine and he props his feet up on his ottoman and takes an hour to relax.

Once he's loose, he rinses his glass and retreats to his bedroom. He promised Aidan a phone call tonight and, honestly, he's not sure who's been looking forward to it more, him or Aidan.

He texts Aidan, *I'm gonna call soon, don't pick up ;)* and gathers all the stuff he needs.

He grabs a towel from the bathroom, lube from his bedside drawer, and sifts through his toy collection until he finds one of his favorite dildos. It's thick and ridged, and he runs two fingers down its length before he leaves his room to grab a few things from his kitchen.

He gets himself a water bottle and a snack, because he knows he'll be too lazy to do it after he comes. He prefers to bask in the afterglow rather than haul himself out of bed to clean up let alone track down something to eat.

He lines everything up on his nightstand then calls Aidan and puts the phone on speaker. His heart thuds with each ring of the phone, expectation growing as Aidan doesn't pick up.

Finally, the phone clicks over to the answering machine, and Aidan's voice filters through. "This is Aidan. I'm unavailable to speak with you right now. Please leave your name, your message, and the number to reach you, and I'll call back as soon as I'm able."

Kyle makes a mental note to give Aidan shit for his message before the phone beeps, and he switches into sex mode.

"Hey," Kyle says, stretching out on his stomach, leaning over his phone. He needs a picture to go with Aidan's contact to give him something to look at when he does this again. "I thought about calling you mid-jerk-off-session, but you deserve the full experience. It means you'll be able to laugh at me for how quickly I come, but I think we both know I'm stupidly easy for you, whether you're in the room with me or not."

Kyle rolls off his bed but stays close enough for the speaker to pick up his voice. "I still have all my clothes on. If you were here then I'd make a show of stripping for you, but you're not, so this'll be quick. Theme of the night, I guess." He laughs as he pulls his T-shirt over his head.

"I've been thinking about this since our phone call this afternoon." He tugs his jeans off next then his boxers. "I didn't get much work done after that. I hope you weren't too distracted giving your lecture."

Kyle's socks are the last piece of clothing to go and those he tosses into his laundry basket. The jeans he can definitely wear again. Maybe the shirt too. Naked now, he runs his hands over his thighs then skims them up his stomach.

He drops back onto his bed, hands and knees this time, and he moves his phone so he won't sweat on it.

"Did your cock jump when you got my text?" Kyle asks. "Did you keep it closed, knowing what it was, but letting the anticipation grow?" He pauses so when he opens the lube, Aidan can hear the click of the cap. "Are you sitting next to your phone waiting for my message to end so you can listen to it? Or are you listening right now? I'm not sure which I like better."

Kyle squeezes some lube onto his hand and wraps that hand around his dick, bracing himself with one arm on the bed and his knees spread wide. He gasps loudly at the first touch of his fingers, loud enough for Aidan to hear through the phone.

He wants Aidan to hear every sound he makes, wants Aidan to feel like he's here with him. He wants Aidan to share in Kyle's pleasure because then it's almost like Kyle's a part of his orgasm. He's vain enough that the thought makes him push his hips into the tight grip of his hand. The lube isn't spread around yet so it's a rough drag that makes him suck in a breath between his teeth.

He strokes himself a few times to make sure he's slick before he fucks his hand again. It's not as good as Aidan's mouth or even his ass would feel around Kyle's dick. That's something they'll have to talk about, whether Aidan's into being fucked.

He groans at the thought of Aidan spread out on his bed, completely naked, on his back with his arms under his head, *waiting*. Waiting to see if Kyle would make it good for him. He would. Kyle would take his time, kissing Aidan's stomach, sucking a bruise on one hip then the other, kissing Aidan's thighs as he opened him up. He'd use one finger until Aidan grew restless and gave Kyle an impatient, demanding look.

When Kyle gave him two fingers, he'd suck his cock, as well, because he isn't good at denying himself the things he wants. And to have his fingers in Aidan and his mouth around him? Definitely something he wants.

He'd have to pull off when he slid three fingers into Aidan, because he'd want to see Aidan's face. To see him flushed and sweating and wanting. Kyle would keep his pace maddeningly slow until Aidan grabbed Kyle's wrist and ordered, "Now."

They'd definitely fuck face to face so Aidan could wrap a hand around the back of Kyle's neck and drag him down for a kiss whenever he wanted one, so he could wrap his legs around Kyle's back and dig his heels into Kyle when he wasn't giving enough.

One of Kyle's favorite things in the world is to feel someone pressed close against him, to have someone *inside* him, and he wants everyone to love it as much as he does. He wants to make Aidan as happy as Aidan makes him.

He—

He has to squeeze the base of his dick to keep from coming, and he's sure his frustrated groan, deep and low, comes through loud and clear over the phone.

He spots his dildo resting precariously on his pillow, and he looks down his body at the hand wrapped around his cock and the flex of his abs every time they contract. He curses quietly to himself.

"I didn't think this through," he confesses. "I'm on my hands and knees, because I know I look good like this and because I can imagine you standing behind me. But it means all I have is my hand on my dick. I can't finger myself until I want to give up touching myself or I move, and I don't want to do either."

He's used his forehead to balance before, knees spread wide, head pressing into his pillow, but it always leaves him with a sore neck.

"Probably for the best," Kyle says. "I didn't ask if I could do more than jerk off, so I'll have to settle for longing looks at my dildo. I'll fuel my fantasies with thoughts of how it would feel in my ass or my mouth."

Kyle arches his back even though there's no one here to see him. "There are ridges on my dildo. I'd push it in slowly so I could feel every one. Spread my legs to give you a view. I'd go as slow as I could stand until I had to fuck myself fast and hard, until all you could hear was me panting for it. Would you be jealous? You wouldn't need to be. If you were here, I'd beg for *you*."

He twists his wrist at the end of his next stroke and that, combined with his thoughts, is almost enough to make him come. He drops his hand from his cock and breathes heavily, head hanging between his shoulders until he pulls back from the edge. He isn't ready to be done, not yet.

"I have a suction dildo I might use next time," Kyle says. "It's one of my favorites. I can stick it to the headboard then call you and choke myself on it as soon as your answering machine picks up."

Kyle would moan around the fake cock so Aidan could hear. Knowing Aidan was on the other side of the line, he'd choke himself until there were tears in his eyes and he'd have to take his hand off his cock so he could wipe them away. He'd break himself apart piece by piece for Aidan to hear and once he was done he'd hang up and wait for Aidan to call and put him back together again.

"Obviously, I wish you were here," Kyle says, and he slides his hand up his stomach to run over his abs, so his fingers can brush over his nipples. He squirms and wishes he could use both his hands, wishes Aidan was here to touch him.

Maybe they can plan a scene where Kyle's on his hands and knees, and it's Aidan's hands touching him. Aidan's hand around his cock and his other hand roaming across Kyle's skin. Kyle tips his head back as though Aidan's there for him to touch. He's disappointed when he looks over his shoulder and sees that he's alone.

"But there's something I like about this too," Kyle continues before he can lose his buzz. "I like that we don't have to be in the same place for me to do something for you."

Kyle stops talking after that, lets Aidan hear his grunts and groans as he careens toward tonight's inevitable end. There's sweat pooling on his back and a flush in his cheeks, and he comes into his fist, breathing hard.

It takes him a few long seconds before he has the energy to sit back on his heels. He wipes his hand on his towel and picks up his phone.

"This is Kyle," he says, voice shaky. "I just left you my message, and you don't need my number, because you can hit callback."

He hangs up and tosses his phone on his bed. He contemplates sprawling across his sheets and calling it a night, but if he cleans up now then he can be in bed for when Aidan calls and he won't have to leave again.

He takes a quick, chilly, shower, wiping off sweat and come, and he's shivering when he comes out of his bathroom. He pulls on his flannel pajama pants and a white cotton T-shirt and settles on his bed again.

His phone is quiet, and he frowns at it, willing it to ring as he takes a sip of water. He breaks off a piece of his granola bar and is still chewing when his phone lights up with a call.

"Hey," Kyle says, picking up before the first ring is through.

He's answered by laughter. "Message critique aside, I enjoyed it."

"Yeah?" Kyle asks. He leans against his pillows and spreads his legs. He slips a hand under the waistband of his pants, palm pressed flat against the inside of his thigh. He thinks idly about wrapping his hand around his cock again but it might be too soon for that. "How much did you like it?"

"I thought about stroking myself in time to what you were doing, but then I thought you'd be disappointed if I didn't let you hear me."

"I would've been. Does that mean you'll touch yourself now?"

"I guess that depends on whether you ask me nicely or not."

Kyle digs his fingers into his thigh as his dick gives a sad, painful twitch. Definitely too soon for him to grow hard again, but he wouldn't mind trying.

And if he can't come, then at least he can listen to Aidan. "Will you come while I'm listening? Please? I want to hear it. All I did was think about you while I touched myself. I thought about your hands on me, thought about your mouth. I thought about you watching me, and if you'd like it. Did you like it? Is that why you're hard right now?"

"You know you're gorgeous, you don't need me to tell you."

"But I want you to. Please?"

"Another time," Aidan promises. "Tonight, I want to hear you."

Kyle can get behind this too. "Yeah? What do you want to hear? You want me to tell you things I didn't say in my message? Or do you want to know what I'd do if I was there with you? I'd put my mouth on you like I did this morning. We're both awake now so you wouldn't let me play. Plus, you've been waiting a while, huh. How patient are you feeling?"

"Are you asking if I'd fuck your mouth?"

"You would but not right away." Kyle grins as he hears Aidan's sharp intake of breath. "You'd slide both your hands through my hair and tug while I swallowed you down because you know how much I like it. But then you'd pull me off your cock because that's something *you* like."

"Is it?" Aidan's voice, normally so smooth and controlled, has a faint tremor in it.

Kyle wants him desperate before their phone call is over. "Me on my knees, straining against the grip in my hair so I can at least get my tongue on your cock? I'd pull against your grip until there were tears in my eyes, but you wouldn't let me closer."

Aidan gasps, a quiet sound barely picked up by the phone, but Kyle hears it. It's proof he *does* know Aidan, and it makes him smile as he takes the fantasy to the next level.

"You'd make me beg," Kyle says, and he slides his hand out of his pants to shove his shirt up. He needs to touch himself, needs to feel skin under his hand even if he wishes he was touching Aidan instead of himself.

"And I would," Kyle says. "I wouldn't be able to tear my gaze away from your cock, how full and heavy and ready it was, but I'd give you my words. I'd tell you how much I needed it back in my mouth, how I'd take anything you gave me. Just the tip at first, my tongue working the head of your cock while you stroked yourself. If I pleased you, then maybe you'd let me lick the whole thing, get you wet enough so I could suck you off again.

"This is where your patience runs out, though. You've been waiting, but you're tired of it. You *want*, and I'm on my knees offering, and so you take. You'd shove my head down and fuck my throat until you came. I'd thank you for it after, my throat raw, my voice shot all to hell, and I'd thank you for making me that way."

Aidan's breathing is rough through the phone, too quick for him to hold out much longer. Kyle shifts on his bed, restless, wishing he was there with Aidan so his fantasy can be reality.

"Please, let me hear you come. I want to know that even when I'm not there, I still bring you pleasure. Please," he says again, voice low, begging, and Aidan exhales sharply.

Aidan's quiet when he comes, low groans, harsh breathing, but no words. It makes Kyle wish they'd agreed to a video call. He feels greedy in the best way—every time Aidan gives him something, Kyle wants more.

And he's allowed to want. He's supposed to.

"Thank you," Aidan says, and warmth blooms in Kyle's chest, spreading outwards until his skin is flushed and there's a smile on his face.

"You…" Kyle trails off, unsure what question he wants to ask.

"I'm quite satisfied," Aidan answers. "You were good for me."

Kyle hums, happy and pleased, and wriggles around until he's tucked under his blankets. "We should do that with video next time. I want to see you."

"Maybe," Aidan says.

Kyle hears him yawn through the phone and he fights off disappointment as he asks, "You need to sleep?"

"Not yet. I'd like to stay on the phone a bit longer, if it's all right with you."

Like Kyle would ever say no to having more of Aidan's time. "Do you want to talk about our plans for tomorrow?"

"Will it be too much of a tease? I'd like it if you didn't come again until I give you permission, but I know that stretches the boundaries of our agreement."

"You want me to wait until tomorrow or does this extend into tomorrow's scene?"

"The first," Aidan answers. "But you don't have to say yes."

"I don't have to say yes to anything," Kyle says, "but I want to. It'll be a little bit like you're here when you're not, your orders keeping me company until I see you tomorrow night."

"That's not too controlling?" Aidan asks, a sliver of doubt in his voice.

"I want it," Kyle promises. "There are lines I won't let you push past, but this isn't one of them. Why don't we talk about tomorrow night, and then I'll tell you how hard thinking about it's made me? I'll even send you a picture, if you want."

Aidan laughs. "And to think *I* was worried about teasing too much."

"Told you, I like it. Now, you wanna hear what else I like?"

Chapter Four

IT'S ALWAYS STRANGE to visit Enchanting Encounters during the day. It's not a complete ghost town—there's usually a handful of people in the café—but the parking lot is mostly empty and all the lights over the bar are dimmed.

There's no one filling the booths, no one jostling for space at the bar, no TJ mixing drinks or grinning at people. There's a sliver of light shining from the door on the far side and that's where he heads.

All the offices are in the rear part of the club, and Kyle certainly doesn't spend equal time in each division of the club, but he's been back here enough to know his way around. He waves at Alicia, the receptionist, and she waves back, phone tucked between her shoulder and her ear which means she can't offer a more vocal greeting.

She does point down the hall and give him a thumbs-up, letting him know Wanda's in her office and expecting him.

Wanda's door is cracked open, and Kyle raps his knuckles on it twice before he pushes the door open. "Hey," he says.

Wanda looks up from her laptop, a marigold scarf with bronze embroidery holding her hair back today. Big earrings hang down from her lobes, heavy enough to make Kyle wince, but they don't seem to bother her.

There are lines on her face that he doesn't remember seeing before, and it's weird to think about Wanda getting older.

She was the first person Kyle met who was *in* the scene. He'd fooled around plenty, not quite sure what he was doing, with people who also weren't sure what they were doing. He knew Jenny, but she was his best friend, and she wasn't involved in the scene so much as a burgeoning photographer. Besides, she knew exactly what she wanted and what she didn't.

Kyle knew what he liked—being on his knees, someone's hands in his hair—but he didn't know how to ask for it. And when he got it, behind bars or in the backs of trucks, he came away with bruised lips and a stinging scalp but missing something he couldn't name.

It was Wanda who took him under her wing and explained to him that there was a difference between rough sex and what he was looking for. It was Wanda who showed him how to ask, and *who* to ask so he didn't end up in a back-alley fight.

Wanda showed him the difference between finding someone who would put him on his knees and someone who made him want to be there. "There's a bigger difference than you might think, between going down and wanting to go down," she'd told him. "Sometimes you'll want one, sometimes you'll want the other. A good Dom will help you figure it out and then give you which one you want. But it's good for *you* to learn too. It'll save everyone a lot of hassle."

Kyle never subbed for her, but she was a mentor to him all the same, and now he's a mentor to others in the club. He still remembers how patient she was with him, how she never made him feel stupid or as if he couldn't look after himself. She guided him until he was ready to be on his own, and now he's trying to pass that kindness on.

Wanda smiles when she sees him. "Hey, yourself. I heard congratulations are in order."

Kyle shrugs but he can't keep the smile off his face. "It's still early, but I'm hopeful."

"Is he good to you?"

Kyle's smile grows. "Yeah."

Wanda's the one who taught Kyle the difference between a Dom talking shit because it's something they both want and one doing it because it makes the Dom feel better. She's the one Kyle went to after his bondage scene went wrong, when he was shaking and scared and convinced *he* was the one who screwed everything up. She's been at his side through his uncertainty, through some of his lowest points, and it makes pride bloom in his chest to be able to share something positive with her.

She knows his long-term goal is to find a serious partner, but Kyle's never found someone who he's clicked with well enough before. But Aidan...Aidan might be the one.

"Good," Wanda says. "Do you want to tell me more about him or do you want to talk business?"

"We'll see how things progress," Kyle says. "I don't want to get ahead of myself. But if this turns into a good thing, you know you're one of the first I'll tell."

"Business it is, then," Wanda says.

Kyle is a big part of the marketing and promotional team for the club. He designs pamphlets and posters and emails, but he also does more involved things. He'll do demos out on the main floor or work with new Doms and he'll talk with any new sub who has questions or just needs someone to listen.

Recently, he worked with Richard, a new Dom, and they were part of a three-person scene; Richard and Kyle together while Renee kept an eye on things. He doesn't scene with new subs in the same way, because he doesn't share well, and the last thing a fledgling sub needs is someone with more experience taking a Dom's attention from them.

Part of being a mentor is knowing his own strengths and weaknesses and playing to his strengths.

Kyle sits in the chair across from Wanda's desk and plays with the hem of his shirt before he says, "I can still do the business side of things, but I'm taking a break from the hands-on stuff for a bit."

Wanda closes her laptop, so she can give Kyle her full attention. "Your decision or his?" she asks as though a part of her will always look out for him like she did when he was young and clueless.

He's still young but not quite so clueless.

"Ours," Kyle answers and Wanda smiles like that was the answer she wanted to hear. "We need some time to figure out what 'us' is. In a few weeks, once we have a better idea of how we work together and what we're both looking for, then I'll bring it up again. Maybe I'll do stuff here again, maybe I won't."

Wanda nods because this is something they've talked about before. Part of his exhibitionism stems from the fact that if he can't get the kind of attention he needs from one person, then he can make up for it by getting bits of attention from a lot of people. But his goal has always been to find one person to be with.

In an ideal world, he'd still do demos at the club, still work with new members, maybe even do some public scenes with his partner, but none of those are things he needs. He can do without if they make his partner uncomfortable and, at least right now, Aidan doesn't seem as open to public play as Kyle is.

"Besides," Kyle continues because he never knows how to stop while he's ahead, "Our arrangement's only for three months. We might be done after that."

Wanda gives him a cutting look. "Don't ruin a good thing before it's even had a chance to happen."

Kyle twists his hands in his T-shirt, stretching it out. "Jenny thinks I should temper my expectations."

"And what do you think?"

"I think I really like him," Kyle answers, "but I think that's exactly why I need to keep my expectations low. Because if it doesn't work..." He shrugs.

"I will throw this at you," Wanda says, holding her stress ball up for him to see. "Allow yourself to be happy. If it ends in three months, then you've had three months where you were in a relationship you enjoyed. And if at the end of three months you continue, it's because you know what the two of you can be together and you want more."

All things Kyle knows, but they sound better coming from someone else. "Anyone ever tell you you're really smart?"

Wanda grins. "Comes with age. But I want to pick your brain about December. We need a theme to build around, and if you suggest anything to do with tinsel bondage then I'm revoking your membership for a month."

"Tinsel?" Kyle winces and crosses his legs. "That would hurt, and not in a good way. But, what we could do is deck the halls with free swinging balls."

Wanda throws her stress ball at Kyle's head and he laughs so hard he falls out of his chair.

WHEN KYLE RETURNS to the club later that night, the bar is full of people and Kyle can barely see TJ's curls as he moves behind the bar, trying to keep everyone happy.

"Flying solo tonight?" Renee asks, winding an arm around Kyle's shoulders.

She's in her favorite boots tonight, the ones that climb up over her knees and are finished with a wicked three-inch heel. Kyle's attention is drawn down to them then up to her face, and she grins at him.

"I already have plans," he says. "Aidan's setting up the room."

"Anything fun?" Renee keeps the arm around his shoulders, but she loses the flirtatious smile.

"Should be. You looking for something tonight? I thought I saw Johnny when I came in."

"Did you?" Renee looks around like she can spot him. "I wouldn't mind an evening with him. Can't let this outfit go to waste. How much setup does your guy need? Can you grab a drink?"

"I'll probably have to leave before we're served." Kyle nods to the bar, even more packed than when he first came in. "TJ's getting a workout tonight."

Renee eyes the bar before she sighs. "Yeah, I should go find Johnny before someone else snaps him up." She presses a kiss to Kyle's cheek. "Have fun tonight."

"You too."

Kyle waves to Lou and chats with Cynthia before he sees another familiar face.

Richard is on the far side of the room, but he's tall enough that he's easy to spot. His muscles strain against the sleeves of his T-shirt. It brings Kyle back to their scene together, how strong Richard had been. When he spots Kyle, his face lights up in a smile. He makes his way through the crowd towards Kyle.

He has a beer, and the glass seems dwarfed in his large hand. A hand Kyle's intimately familiar with. His gaze must linger too long, because when he glances up at Richard's face, the man's expression has shifted from friendly to interested.

"Yeah?" Richard asks.

"Uh, no, sorry," Kyle says, wincing. "I have plans for the night, but, uh—" He gestures to Richard's full figure. "Just reminiscing."

Richard's disappointed look is quickly replaced with one of satisfaction. "That good?"

Kyle pokes Richard's chest. "You're fishing for compliments. That's *my* job."

Richard laughs, deep and rumbling. "You look casual tonight."

"That's the nice thing about arranging a scene in advance, I don't have to try as hard."

"Bullshit," Richard says.

"But it sounded good." It's Kyle's turn to laugh as he tugs on the plain black T-shirt he's wearing. "How about this one; I'm going to lose my clothes as soon as I walk into the room so it doesn't matter what I'm wearing?"

Richard's gaze dips down, his eyes darkening as he considers Kyle naked.

Kyle grins and hooks his thumbs in his back pockets to make his shirt pull tight against his chest. "Now, who's reminiscing?"

"It was a good scene. I've done a couple since, nothing in public, but maybe once I'm more confident. I liked knowing everyone was watching."

"It's a good feeling," Kyle agrees. "Are you looking for something in particular tonight?"

"You're playing matchmaker?"

Kyle shrugs. "I'm always willing to give you a nudge toward someone I think you'll play well with. I shouldn't be the only one having fun tonight."

"I'm mingling tonight. I mean, I wouldn't turn something down if it sounded good, but Renee said it's important to be part of the community, so I'm communing."

"I'm not sure that's the word you want." Kyle laughs and pulls his phone out of his pocket because it's buzzing at him.

AIDAN: *Ready for you. Room 4.*

"Leaving?" Richard guesses.

KYLE: *On my way.*

Kyle slips his phone back into his pocket. "That obvious?"

"Little bit," Richard says. "Is this the kind of thing I wish you luck for?"

Kyle laughs again and goes up on his toes to pat Richard's cheek. "I don't need luck."

"Have fun, then?"

"Oh, I definitely will," Kyle promises before he heads downstairs and to the private rooms.

Chapter Five

IT'S A STRUGGLE to walk instead of run, because he knows where Aidan is, knows he's waiting for Kyle, and knows exactly what's going to happen once he's there. They're playing out last night's scene, except Aidan will be there in the room instead of just a voice through the phone.

Kyle will put on a show, but this time there'll be an audience, and he doesn't want to wait any more.

He knocks on the door of Room 4 because he doesn't have a key and when Aidan opens it, he stands in the doorway, taking up enough space that Kyle would have to contort himself to get by. He takes the hint and stays where he is.

"Look at me," Aidan says.

Kyle's mouth goes dry as he lifts his gaze to Aidan's face. So, *this* is the kind of night it'll be. They've talked about Aidan micromanaging scenes, and how Kyle has to be in the right mindset for it, because most of the time he likes a little wiggle room, likes to mouth off and be pushy.

But sometimes he likes someone to take complete control, and tonight's shaping up to be one of those nights. Aidan's gaze isn't hard, but there's no give in it. He and Kyle have talked about what they each want out of the night and Aidan knows Kyle's hard limits, which means the rest of tonight is up to Aidan.

Kyle doesn't need to worry, he doesn't need to anticipate what will happen. All he has to do is let it happen. Aidan will take care of everything.

Take care of *him*.

Kyle's eyes almost slip shut before he catches the movement at the last second. He sways toward Aidan who steadies him with a hand on his hip and another curving under his chin.

"There you go," Aidan says, low, pleased, and he squeezes Kyle's hip before he steps aside so Kyle can come in.

Kyle stumbles through the doorway more than he steps through it, but he keeps his balance as Aidan reaches behind him to pull the door closed. Kyle hasn't gone down this easy in—well, he doesn't know how long. He could fight it, but he doesn't see any reason why he should. Aidan's safe, someone Kyle can trust to make decisions for both of them.

"Color?" Aidan asks.

"Green," Kyle answers. "This is good."

"Let me know if it's too much."

Kyle nods.

Aidan curls his fingers around Kyle's wrist, and it takes him a moment to realize why it feels weird. He isn't wearing his cuffs. They decided on using them to mark a scene when they're not at Enchanting Encounters with its private spaces and clearly marked boundaries. Kyle hadn't thought to bring them tonight, and now he regrets it.

His wrists are bare.

The touch of Aidan's skin against his is good, but it's not enough. Maybe Aidan will grip him tighter, leave the imprint of his touch when he inevitably lets go. Maybe he'll even leave red marks or bruises behind to remind Kyle that Aidan's here and holding him together.

Kyle doesn't realize he's stopped moving until Aidan tips his chin up so they're looking at each other.

"Too much?" Aidan asks, a hint of concern in his eyes.

"It's good. But I'm going to go deep." He can feel it already, a wave of comfort and security and *rightness* that wants to pull him down, and he wants nothing more than to let it happen, but he has to consider Aidan's needs too. "You need to tell me now if you don't want that."

Aidan's thumb brushes across Kyle's cheek, almost too gentle for Kyle to stand. He wants to turn away from the touch, wants to fold into it. His eyelashes flutter as his eyes threaten to close, but he keeps his gaze on Aidan, waiting for his answer.

"I want it," Aidan says, stumbling over his words. He flushes as though eagerness is something to be embarrassed of.

Kyle turns his head to press a kiss against the tip of Aidan's thumb.

Aidan walks backward as he leads Kyle past the couch and the solid wooden desk and into the bedroom. There's a door on the far wall leading to the bathroom, but most of the bedroom is taken up by a large king-size bed.

The covers are already stripped back, and there's a hand towel and a bottle of lube on the nightstand, a similar setup to what Kyle had last night.

"You still good to show me what you did last night?"

Kyle nods then says, "Yes," for good measure.

Aidan lingers at Kyle's side for a moment before he sits on a chair pulled up close to the bed. "Strip."

Kyle eagerly pops the button on his pants and has them halfway to his knees before Aidan shakes his head. He freezes and wonders what he's done wrong.

"Slower," Aidan says. He leans back in his chair and stretches his legs out, making himself comfortable. "You like to be watched. Give me something worth watching."

Kyle's breath catches in his throat and color floods his cheeks. He pulls his pants back up with shaking hands and somehow fastens his zipper again. It takes him two tries to push the button back through the hole.

Aidan wants a show, and Kyle desperately wants to give him one, but he doesn't know where to start.

"Tell me what you want," Kyle says. "Please. I want to be what you want."

Aidan's expression softens as he takes in Kyle, standing next to the bed, lost and a little confused, defeated by something he's done hundreds of times before. Kyle knows how to take his clothes off, but he doesn't know how Aidan wants it, and tonight Kyle wants to be perfect.

"Shirt first," Aidan says, his voice steady and soothing away worries Kyle didn't even know he had. "Hold the collar and pull it over your head."

Kyle pulls his shirt over his head and lets it drop to the floor beside him. He glances at Aidan, wondering if he's about to be scolded for being messy, but Aidan isn't staring at the discarded shirt. He's staring at Kyle's chest, his gaze dipping down to Kyle's belly button then dragging back up over the plane of his chest.

"You've been working out," Aidan says.

Kyle nods, even though it wasn't a question. "I like it. And I want you to want to look at me."

"I do," Aidan promises. "I'm looking at you right now. I plan on looking at you all night."

Kyle blushes, color sweeping up into his cheeks and down across his chest. He fights the urge to cover himself, even though this is what he wants. Even though he's worn less in front of tmore people and didn't feel an ounce of shame. Not that shame is what he feels now. He feels *vulnerable*, like he's opening himself up to Aidan and he's not sure what Aidan will do with him.

He's safe, Kyle reminds himself. *I wouldn't trust myself to him if he wasn't. He'll take care of me.*

"Shoes next," Aidan says. "Left shoe first, bring your foot up to your hands. I don't want you to hide your chest now that you've taken your shirt off for me."

Kyle obeys, the certainty and specificity in Aidan's voice helping to ground him.

"Good," Aidan says when Kyle drops his left shoe to the floor. "Left sock now."

Kyle strips down, one article of clothing at a time, following Aidan's instructions the whole way. Once Kyle's naked, Aidan directs him to the bed, where he gets on his hands and knees, same as he did last night.

Aidan doesn't move from his chair, and when Kyle hangs his head between his arms, he can't see the man even in his peripheral vision.

"I want to see what I couldn't see last night," Aidan says. "I want to see you touch yourself, knowing I'm watching this time, that I'm in the room to see every reaction you have, no matter how big or how small it is."

"I'm not sure I can talk like I did last night," Kyle admits. He's in a different place now than he was then. He's sunk deeper into himself, and he doesn't want to try to fight how he's feeling. He still wants to show off, still wants to display himself, but there's something softer about tonight's need.

Last night, he had to make up for the fact that Aidan wasn't with him. He wanted to make Aidan wish they weren't in separate places. But tonight, he has Aidan, which means all Kyle has to do is enjoy himself while Aidan watches.

"I'll talk for you," Aidan says.

"Thank you."

Kyle lifts his head and looks over at where Aidan's still sitting in his chair. He leans forward like he's going to join Kyle on the bed or maybe kiss him. Kyle holds his breath, waiting, but then Aidan settles back into his chair.

Kyle's chest hurts, weighed down with disappointment, but he doesn't push for more the way he might on a different night. Aidan has a plan, and Kyle needs to trust it.

He looks back at the teal sheets beneath him.

"I—" Kyle glances at Aidan again. "Please?" He's not even sure what he's asking for, but he knows Aidan will give him what he needs. He sinks deeper into his own head, pulling back from what's around him until there is only his body arranged on the bed and the steady pressure of Aidan's gaze on his skin.

"Lube," Aidan says, voice low to keep from disturbing whatever spell he's woven throughout the room. "I don't want you to chafe."

Kyle shifts his weight so he can support himself on one arm and he reaches for the lube. He flicks the cap open one-handed but struggles to squeeze it onto his hand without leaving the position Aidan's put him in or making a mess.

Heat floods his face, He's embarrassed because he can't figure out this one simple task, and if Aidan would just help him—

Aidan *could* help, but he isn't. It means he wants to watch Kyle struggle. He won't judge Kyle for making a mess or taking longer than he normally would. Aidan would step in if Kyle did something he didn't want which means the struggle is part of Aidan's plan.

He finally manages a palmful of lube, and he wraps his hand around his cock to spread it around. It squelches and maybe he has a little too much, but he likes the mess. He likes when there's too much lube and everything's slippery, how it changes the sounds of being fucked. He likes how his partner has to hold him tighter or risk losing their grip.

What he likes more than lube, though, is come. He wonders how long he'll have to wait before he can ask Aidan to come on his face or his thighs. Kyle loves when, at the end of the night, he's panting, sweat and come cooling on his skin. He likes being marked even if some of those marks will wash away in the post-scene shower.

Tonight, with Aidan all the way in his chair, Kyle won't have come streaked across his skin unless it's his own. He doesn't even have Aidan's hands on him. He has Aidan's gaze, has his full attention, and maybe Kyle's greedy, but he wants more.

He whines, low in his throat, and reaches his hand out toward Aidan. Aidan promised to take care of him tonight, promised that if Kyle gave himself over, then he would receive everything he needs. And Kyle needs. He turns words over in his head, searching for the right ones.

He hears the drag of the chair against the carpet before one of Aidan's hands rests on his calf. It isn't an erogenous zone, but it's contact, and Kyle relaxes into the touch. If he can't see Aidan, then he needs to be touched by him, needs to know he's here and not on the other side of a phone call.

"I'm here," Aidan promises. "I've got you.'

"Will you talk?" Last night, Kyle narrated everything he was doing, because Aidan wasn't in the room with him, but tonight Aidan's here. Kyle doesn't need to talk tonight, and if he did, then he thinks it would pull him out of his headspace.

"Of course." Aidan slides his hand up to the inside of Kyle's knee then down to his ankle, squeezing briefly as he curls his fingers around Kyle's skin. "You painted quite the picture for me last night, but tonight I want to see you."

"It'd be easier if I was on my back." Kyle can't imagine there's a good view like this, unless Aidan's into the flex of Kyle's shoulders or something.

"I want to see you like this."

Well, then. Kyle strokes himself again and thinks that maybe he used too much lube, because his cock slips through his fist too quickly. He wipes his hand across his stomach, cleaning it the best he can.

"I have a towel," Aidan says, amused.

"I like the mess."

"Maybe when you're done I'll have you turn onto your back so I can see the mess you've made of yourself. Lube and come on your chest, a flush in your cheeks, pleasure written into the lazy sprawl of your limbs."

"Is that what *you* like?"

"I like you," Aidan answers. "And I'll like knowing you're disheveled because I asked for it. I'm barely touching you, but I'm still the reason you're finding your pleasure tonight."

Kyle drops his head to the pillows, unable to hold himself up anymore. Aidan knows exactly what to say to hit him the hardest. With every word, every touch, Kyle unravels more. He's not sure what state he'll be in by the end of the night, but he does know Aidan will put him back together as gently as he takes him apart.

"You're stunning," Aidan says, the admiration in his voice too much for Kyle to handle right now.

He can demand attention, he can court it, but when it's given freely like this...Kyle shakes his head. He's too deep, too willing to believe everything he hears.

"Yes," Aidan says, firm, no room for Kyle to doubt him. "You are. I know you work hard at it, and all your work should be appreciated. When I listened to your message, I tried to picture what you looked like, but I didn't do you justice."

Kyle can't help but arch his back, *show off*, and Aidan laughs as he skims his fingers over Kyle's skin again.

"I promise you, I'm looking," Aidan says. "Maybe I should take a video so I don't have to rely on my imagination next time."

Kyle's rhythm stutters at the thought of Aidan filming him. His face heats and his hand works faster, almost desperate.

"I could keep it as a reminder of tonight, something to pull up whenever you aren't around. Create my own personal collection of porn."

Kyle groans and presses his mouth against his skin to muffle the sound so he won't miss anything Aidan says.

"But I don't need a video, do I?" Aidan asks. "Because I can have you like this whenever I want. All I have to do is ask."

Kyle nods, too far gone for words. He wouldn't say no to Aidan taking videos of him, and he definitely won't say no to Aidan wanting him like this every morning. Maybe every evening. Will this be what it's like when they scene at each other's apartments? Will Kyle wait for Aidan to come home from work, sprawled across the couch or the bed, ready to be used any way Aidan wants?

Kyle strokes himself faster, harder, as if he's racing himself to orgasm. He's right on the edge, and he could tip himself over with a well-placed touch or twist of his wrist, but he wants Aidan's voice to make him come.

"Come for me," Aidan says, permission and order rolled into one, and that's what does it. Kyle groans as he spills into his fist. He rolls onto his back, exhausted but wanting to see Aidan, wanting to know if he's pleased him.

Aidan's eyes are dark but alert, tracking Kyle's movement as he stretches out across the bed and, after a glance at his hand, wipes his come on his stomach.

"There's a towel," Aidan reminds him.

Kyle lifts one shoulder in a shrug which is about all the movement he's capable of right now. "You can add to the mess."

Kyle's not up to anything coordinated at the moment, but he wouldn't mind Aidan jerking off on him. And he really wouldn't mind if Aidan fucked him. He likes being fucked right after he's come, he likes how it rides the edge of too much, likes how it's not about him at all. He runs his fingers through the mess on his stomach and spreads his legs invitingly.

"No fucking tonight," Aidan says. "But I wouldn't mind adding to your mess."

"Please?"

Aidan smiles as he slings a leg over Kyle's torso so he's straddling him. Aidan's still in all his clothes, and Kyle wants to protest, but Aidan holds a finger to Kyle's lips as he pops the button on his pants one-handed.

Kyle settles back against the pillows, chastised. Aidan promised he had a plan, and Kyle promised to see it through. He just wishes he could see *Aidan*.

"You're gorgeous," Aidan says as he pulls himself out of his pants.

Kyle's gaze immediately drops to Aidan's cock, fully hard, a bit of wetness smeared around the tip. His mouth parts, *wanting*, and Aidan rests his finger against Kyle's tongue.

"Is this what you want?"

Kyle sucks on Aidan's finger in answer, and his eyes slip half-shut as his post-orgasm stupor hits him hard. He doesn't shut his eyes all the way, because he doesn't want to lose sight of Aidan, but he's drifting.

"There you go," Aidan says, pleased, as if Kyle's exactly what he wants. "Lay there and let me look at you. Let me—" He groans as he comes on Kyle's stomach.

Kyle grins, pleased, and runs his fingers through the mess. It makes him feel claimed, gives him something to cling do as Aidan eases himself off the bed.

"Will you be okay if I grab us a washcloth?"

Kyle nods.

When Aidan returns, he's in his boxers and his undershirt, and he uses the damp, warm washcloth to wipe the come and lube off Kyle's skin. It feels a little like Aidan's wiping himself away, scraping Kyle bare, and he can't help his whine when Aidan steps away.

"I was going to return this to the bathroom," Aidan says, but he doesn't move. "Do you want me to stay?"

Kyle nods. A part of him knows Aidan will be back. He's a good Dom, and there isn't anywhere else for him to go, but without his cuffs and without the evidence of what they did, Kyle feels too vulnerable to let Aidan out of his sight.

"All right," Aidan says. "Do you want any of your clothes?"

"Boxers."

Aidan helps Kyle into them and then they lie down in bed together, Kyle immediately draping himself over Aidan as if to keep him here.

"We're spending the night here," Aidan says as he runs a hand through Kyle's hair. "And then tomorrow we'll be at your place or mine. You went deep tonight, and I want to be with you tomorrow."

Kyle certainly won't turn down more time with Aidan. He turns his head to press a kiss against Aidan's neck. "Will you finally get naked tomorrow?"

Aidan laughs. "Maybe."

That's a no. Kyle grumbles, but it's too much effort to be annoyed right now so he lets it go and burrows closer to Aidan instead.

Chapter Six

KYLE'S WOKEN UP by Aidan trying to slide out of bed, and it's too early for Kyle to be awake and certainly too early for him to be awake and alone. He throws an arm and a leg over Aidan to keep him in bed.

"No," he adds for extra measure.

Aidan laughs as he eases Kyle to his side of the bed. "I won't be gone long."

Kyle scowls at Aidan's back and, in retribution, wraps all the blankets around himself. But that means he overheats, so he kicks them all off then he's chilly so by the time Aidan returns from the bathroom, Kyle's sitting up and rubbing his eyes.

"We can still sleep," Aidan says, but he looks too awake to be able to sleep again.

Kyle wouldn't mind a lazy morning full of cuddling, but he's hungry, and he'd rather cuddle in his own bed or Aidan's than the one here at Enchanting Encounters. He stretches out across the bed, grinning as Aidan's gaze is drawn to his bare chest.

"Are you trying to tempt me back into bed?" Aidan asks.

Kyle wasn't but sees the potential. "Is it working?"

Aidan laughs again and pats his knee. "Are you hungry? I'm sure the café is open."

"Oh, no," Kyle says, sliding out of bed and finding where he dropped his clothes last night. They're a little rumpled, but they'll be fine for a quick drive home. "You said we're spending the day together, which means I'm in charge of feeding us. Whose place are we going to?"

"Mine?" Aidan suggests. "You haven't seen it yet, and all my teaching stuff is there. I was hoping to do some work today."

"I probably should too. Can we swing by my place first so I can grab my laptop and make breakfast and then we'll stop at the store on the way to yours?" Kyle scratches at his stomach and adds, "I should probably grab a quick shower while I'm home."

"Or you can pack a bag and shower at my place," Aidan says.

"Yeah?" A slow smile spreads across Kyle's face. "Can't wait to get me naked in your home?"

"Something like that." Aidan holds out a hand. "Come on, I was promised food."

KYLE ENDS UP taking a quick shower at his apartment, because he doesn't want to wear wrinkled clothes to Aidan's, and he doesn't want to change into clean clothes when he's dirty. He leaves Aidan in the kitchen, showers quickly, and when he's done, Aidan has coffee made for the two of them.

"I can toast a mean bagel," Aidan says, handing Kyle a mug full of coffee, "but it sounded like you have other plans."

"No bagels today." Kyle accepts the coffee and makes sure their fingers brush on the handoff. He takes a sip of his coffee as he wanders over to his fridge. He starts them off with small bowls of yogurt, granola, and fresh fruit to tide them over while he fries some eggs and makes toast. It's not the most interesting food he's ever made, but hopefully he'll have other opportunities to do breakfast with him.

They wash their dishes side by side, bumping elbows and grinning stupidly at each other, and when they kiss they both taste like coffee. Kyle's almost tempted to curl his hand in Aidan's shirt and drag him back to his bedroom and stay there all day, but Aidan said he wanted to do some work, and Kyle has to admit he's interested in seeing where Aidan lives.

STOP & SHOP is fairly crowded, because apparently Saturday morning is a peak shopping time, but Kyle navigates them around kids racing their carts down the aisles and babies throwing things overboard and women in yoga pants and high ponytails who navigate the aisles as if they're on a mission.

Kyle lingers in front of the tortillas, because there are at least five different sizes to choose from. He knows exactly what he wants to make for lunch and dinner, and he wants to make enough so Aidan will have leftovers throughout the week.

He likes the idea of filling Aidan's fridge with Tupperware for him to bring to work or heat up for dinner so that even when Kyle isn't with him, there's something to remind Aidan of him.

There might be a problem with his plan, though. "Please tell me you have a 9x13 pan," Kyle says.

"I do. Perfect size for brownies."

Kyle grabs a big pack of tortillas and moves on to the enchilada sauces. "On a scale of one to five, how would you rate your adventurousness?"

Aidan points to the mildest of them. "I prefer to keep my adventurousness out of the kitchen."

Kyle grins as he plucks two cans off the shelf. They move on to rice next, then chicken, where he has to pause to figure out which looks the best.

"There's a whole frozen section," Aidan says, leaning over Kyle's shoulder, possibly to annoy him, possibly to distract him. "Some of it already comes pre-breaded."

"No," Kyle says. "But if you like breaded chicken, then I can make Cheez-It chicken for you sometime. You can't get *that* in a bag in the freezer section."

"Definitely not."

Kyle finally picks the tray of chicken breasts he wants, but as he grabs a plastic bag to wrap it in, Aidan puts a hand on his arm.

"You know you don't have to do this, right?"

Kyle smiles—it's impossible not to—and presses a brief kiss to Aidan's cheek. "I know, but I like it."

Aidan eyes the raw chicken and takes a step back. "I guess someone has to. No ground beef, though. It doesn't look right."

"Okay," Kyle says and drags Aidan over to the cheese section.

It isn't until they're leaving the store that Kyle realizes another potential problem. "Please tell me you have a Crockpot. I can do dinner without one, but it'll be easier with it."

"I think my mom bought me one for Christmas one year. You plug it into the wall, right?"

"We'll take a picture of you using it for her," Kyle says. "But, fair warning, if it's still in the box then I'm going to laugh at you."

NOT ONLY IS the Crockpot still in the box, the box is still taped up. Kyle laughs so hard Aiden leaves him in the kitchen to fetch his schoolwork.

"I would apologize," Kyle says when Aidan returns, "but I wouldn't actually mean it."

Aidan spreads his things on the island counter, a stack of unread papers in one pile and read papers in a second. He lines up two red pens next to the unread papers and holds a third in his hand, and he uses it to point as he says, "I'm great with the microwave, and I've gotten better at 'add to a pot of boiling water and watch for ten minutes.' It's not like I starve."

Kyle opens the freezer to show off the neat stacks of frozen pot pies. "It's like you're still in college. You realize you're in a house, right?"

"A house owned by the college. I almost rented an apartment, but it felt too much like a dorm room, and I was glad to put those behind me."

"Oh?" Kyle asks as he washes potatoes. "Sounds like there's a story here. Roommate who smoked up all the time and set off the fire alarm for the building? Never did his laundry so the room smelled like stale beer and BO?"

Aidan sets his pen down, apparently giving up on work before he even begins. "My freshman year roommate was part of the movement on my floor to get around the no-pet policy."

Kyle places the potatoes in a pot of water to boil then soften as he preps the rest of the ingredients for baked potato soup. "Let me guess, it ended well?"

"The RA knew something was up so there were room inspections, but they were always announced which led to a ridiculous kitten-smuggling system. Eventually, someone's mom took pity on the poor creature and brought him home to raise. Dave, my roommate, is the one who put the kitten in the box outside the window, because he forgot the RA was coming by."

"Good job, Dave."

"He now has two young daughters. And I know it's been years since college, but all I can think every time I see pictures of them is that I hope he never put them in a box outside a window."

"My freshman roommate would jerk off into his socks and then not wash them," Kyle says. "When I brought it up to him he told me the smell always went away after a few days and it'd be fine. I think I traumatized him when I explained the smell went away because his mom either washed his socks or threw them out."

"Did he ever do it while you were in the room?"

"Ugh. Yes. I guess I have to give him credit, because he at least made an effort to wait until I was asleep, but he was loud. Like, wake me up kind of loud, and I was not into his heavy breathing and awkward grunting."

"Which means you had a roommate you were into." Aidan rests his elbows on the counter and leans forward, papers forgotten.

Kyle shrugs but he can't quite keep the smile off his face. "Yeah, senior year I ended up with a random roommate, because all the guys I'd lived with before graduated. George was also a senior, and he'd jerk it in the room sometimes. But he'd do it before I had a chance to fall asleep or when I said I'd be out, but he waited long enough that I'd have a good chance of walking in on him. To be fair, it took me longer than it should have to realize he was doing it on purpose."

Aidan laughs. "Someone less subtle than you? What'd you do when you figured it out?"

"I asked him if he liked me walking in on him or watching him more." Kyle grins. "The rest of that year turned out to be pretty fun."

"I'll bet."

Kyle dumps everything into the Crockpot and puts the lid on before he sets it to high. He pulls his laptop out of his bag and sits down next to Aidan at the counter.

"Is it productive time?" Kyle asks.

Aidan glances at his papers and sighs. "I have to get this done for Monday, which means I could put it off until tomorrow, but—"

"That'll be a sucky Sunday. Which means we'll be productive until it's time to start lunch and then we can swap more stories while I make the enchiladas."

"Wait." Aidan's gaze is drawn to the Crockpot. "Isn't that lunch?"

Kyle shakes his head.

"You're making it first! Shouldn't that mean we eat it first?"

"Crockpots are magic, but they need time to work their magic. Soup is for dinner."

"This is why cooking is stupid," Aidan mutters as he picks up his first paper.

Kyle opens his laptop and manages to settle into his own work. It helps that he's interested in the project he's working on. It's the library's next big event, and one of Charlotte's favorite, *Blind Date with a Book*. Kyle doesn't understand the appeal in dressing up and eating with a mystery book, but he doesn't have to understand, he just has to design the advertisements for it.

So far, all he has is a woman eating spaghetti *Lady and the Tramp*-style with a book, but he hasn't given the book a title yet. *Silence of the Lambs* is the first title that jumps into his head, and he laughs too hard for it to be a good idea. Still, it doesn't take long to throw some text on the book and send the picture off to Charlotte so she can have a laugh too.

"Really?" Aidan asks, looking over Kyle's shoulder.

"I have to amuse myself somehow. I won't actually use this. Maybe I'll give her a glass of wine and *The Grapes of Wrath*."

Aidan groans.

"Come on," Kyle says, nudging him. "Get into the *spirits* of things."

"I will push you off your chair. Don't think I won't."

Kyle keeps laughing as he edits a glass of wine into the picture.

BY THE TIME Kyle sets his work aside to start lunch, the smell of creamy soup has begun to spread through the kitchen.

Aidan looks up from the paper he's on, but Kyle shakes his head. "Don't let me interrupt you if you're working."

"You're cooking for me, I can keep you company."

"I'm cooking for *us*." Kyle takes the chicken out of the fridge. "Where would I find a cutting board and appropriately sharp knives?"

"The cutting board is under the oven with the baking sheets, and the knives are in the silverware drawer." The last bit is said more like a question as if Aidan doesn't know where else a person would keep their knives.

"I have a knife stand," Kyle explains as he grabs the cutting board and sifts through the drawer for the knife he wants. "It works as a knife holder and it keeps them sharp." He finally finds something with more of an edge than a butter knife, and he plucks the two green peppers off the counter. He slices the first pepper in half and digs out the seeds. "Do you have a garbage disposal?"

"Even better, compost. It's by the sink."

"Huh." Kyle dumps the pepper innards in the small bin by the sink before he cuts open the second pepper. "I didn't peg you for a compost guy."

"Ritchie, the guy I share the duplex with, is. He's an environmental science professor with a focus in sustainability. Hence, the compost."

"Do you have a garden, then?" Kyle asks as he cuts the peppers into thin, even strips.

"Ritchie does. I give him my banana peels, and he knows better than to give me anything that comes out of his garden."

Kyle laughs as he slices the peppers into thin strips and dumps them in the skillet. He moves onto the chicken next and adds it to the peppers before turning the stovetop on. He leans against the counter so he can watch Aidan work while the skillet sizzles.

Aidan's staring at a paper again, his pen tapping against his lips. He nods like he agrees with a point his student's made, and Kyle sees Aidan's first smile since he began grading.

"Kenzie never disappoints me," Aidan says, scrawling something Kyle assumes is complimentary. "It's a shame she isn't an art history major."

"Is she taking the class for fun?"

Kyle turns the peppers and the chicken so they'll cook evenly, and it sends another burst of flavor into the air. His stomach rumbles even though they ate pretty recently.

"She's a biology major who enjoys arguing and being right. She'll take humanities classes when she has the credits to spare so she can write long, detailed papers on why her point of view is the best one. But her dad will stop co-signing her loans if she makes it even her minor, so she just takes classes here and there."

"I know how that one goes," Kyle says.

"Your parents didn't approve of your major?"

"I'm not sure my dad's ever approved of anything I've done." Kyle pokes at the skillet again. "My stepdad thinks I'm some kind of technological wizard, but since he's still forwarding chain emails from an AOL account, I'm not sure his opinion counts."

"Chain emails?" Aidan asks, picking up on the lighter of the confessions Kyle made. "That's a throwback."

"No kidding."

"My dad's after me to follow him on Twitter like it'll make him Twitter-famous, but all he does is live-tweet his workday."

Kyle laughs as he turns the peppers and chicken over one last time.

"Have you ever stuffed an enchilada?" Kyle asks.

Aidan raises his eyebrows. "Is that a euphemism?"

"Not this time." Kyle grins and opens the fridge to grab the rest of the ingredients. "You want to learn?"

"Sure," Aidan says.

Chapter Seven

ONCE THE ENCHILADAS are nestled in their pan, Kyle puts them in the oven and sets the timer for sixty minutes.

"This is another reason I don't bother with real food," Aidan says, pointing at the timer. "It takes too long. When I decide I'm hungry, I want to eat."

"Which is why you cook before you're hungry." Kyle leans against the counter and smiles at Aidan's pout. "Why don't you shower? That'll kill twenty minutes or so, and I'll think of some other way to pass the rest of the time."

"Some way?" Aidan asks.

Kyle grins and pushes off the counter, and Aidan spreads his legs so Kyle can step into the space between them. "You want a preview?" He rests one hand on Aidan's thigh and curls the other around his neck. They're close enough all Kyle has to do is lean in if he wants their lips to touch, but he waits for Aidan's nod before he does it.

Honestly, Kyle means it to be a quick kiss, a promise of what's waiting for Aidan after his shower, but once he starts kissing Aidan, he doesn't want to stop. Aidan doesn't take charge. He lets Kyle slide his hand into his hair to tilt his head for a better angle, and when Kyle nips at Aidan's bottom lip, he doesn't pull away.

He gasps, mouth parting, and Kyle squeezes Aidan's thigh before he bites at him again, a little harder this time. Aidan groans and he wraps his legs around Kyle's waist, pulling him closer as if Kyle has anywhere else he wants to be.

"You like that?" Kyle asks even though it's obvious. "Wonder where else you like to be bitten." He ducks his head so he can graze his teeth down Aidan's neck, hard enough to make him shudder, but light enough he won't leave any marks.

He knows why he can't leave hickeys or bruises anywhere that can't be covered by a shirt, the same reason Aidan can't leave them on Kyle, but it's tempting. Kyle wants to suck a bruise right under Aidan's jaw or bite at his neck until a bruise blooms across his skin, an obvious sign that says *Back off: I'm taken.*

"This, ah, this is a preview?" Aidan asks.

"I might've gotten carried away," Kyle admits. He pulls back enough to appreciate the flush across Aidan's cheeks and how his bottom lip is a touch puffier than it was earlier. Kyle's tempted to lean in for another kiss, but he knows if he does, then it'll be even harder to stop. "But you could postpone your shower."

Aidan glances at the kitchen timer. "That's not enough time to do everything I want with you, and I won't want to pause when lunch is ready. Another point against cooking, by the way."

Kyle laughs and when Aidan relaxes his legs, Kyle's able to step away from him. "Fine. Shower and leave me here all alone."

"After lunch," Aidan promises.

Kyle nods and opens the computer, hoping to do a bit more work while Aidan isn't here to distract him.

He makes it through his email before he hears footsteps from the wrong direction. He twists in his chair to see a middle-aged man in a pair of faded jeans and a T-shirt with two cartoon people digging through a garden and the words *Let's get dirty* beneath them.

"Ritchie?" Kyle guesses.

"That's me." The man frowns. "Uh, should I know you? I'm sorry, I'm not good with names."

"We haven't met, but Aidan talks about you. I'm Kyle."

"It smells incredible in here, which I assume is your doing."

"Yeah, lunch is in the oven." Kyle glances toward the hallway as if Aidan will show up and rescue him. "Uh, do you want to eat with us?"

"As long as you did the cooking." Ritchie laughs and makes himself at home in the kitchen, grabbing a beer out of the fridge and plopping himself down at the island. "I thought I heard Aidan laughing and, I mean, it wouldn't be the first time I walked in on him talking to himself, but you were a pleasant surprise."

Kyle smiles, a touch forced, and hopes Aidan cuts his shower short. Normally, Kyle is great at small talk. He's friendly, he's outgoing, and people tend to like him, but this is different. This is one of Aidan's coworkers, and Kyle isn't sure how to act. Is Aidan out? Will Ritchie assume they're dating? Should Kyle roll with it if he does?

"You have a garden?" Kyle asks.

Ritchie lights up and forgets entirely about his beer as he talks about composting and gardens and vegetables and whether watermelon is worth the hassle, and Kyle doesn't have to say another word until Aidan joins them in the kitchen.

"Oh," Aidan says, stopping short when he sees them. "Hey, Ritchie."

Ritchie lifts his beer in greeting. "I'm crashing your place for lunch. Apparently, you managed to find a friend who knows his way around the kitchen." He wanders away from the island to lift the top off the Crockpot. "Mm, nothing better than hot soup in the fall."

"That's dinner," Aidan says. "Lunch is in the oven. Kyle's a good cook."

Kyle grins at the praise and, once Ritchie's bent over to look in the oven, he blows Aidan a kiss.

Ritchie whistles as he peeks under the tinfoil. "You're going to spoil him. And that's a shit-ton of enchiladas. Are you having a party? And you didn't invite me?"

"No party," Kyle answers. "I wanted leftovers so Aidan had something to eat for the rest of the week. I didn't think to ask if he had Tupperware, though."

"I have Tupperware," Aidan says. "You're not as funny as you think you are."

"That is blatantly false."

Ritchie shuts the oven. "First time over?" He looks alarmed. "Are you the new English guy?"

Aidan sighs. "Professor *Elizabeth* Jefferson is a visiting professor, who won't be here until next semester."

"And it's still first semester." Ritchie nods to himself. "Good."

Kyle's still trying to figure out how open Aidan is with his colleagues when someone else comes into the kitchen. She's in a long-sleeved shirt with a soccer ball on it, and she covers a yawn with her hand as she wanders into the room.

"There you are," she says, slinging an arm over Ritchie's shoulders. "You said you were popping out to the garden, but you never came back."

"We've been invited for lunch," Ritchie tells her.

"Have we?" The woman looks from Kyle, sitting at the island, his computer still open, to Aidan, standing in the entryway where he hasn't budged since spotting Ritchie.

"Well, I was," Ritchie says, "but I'm sure if Kyle knew you were awake then he would've invited you."

"Or known who I was." The woman smiles and pats Ritchie's cheek as if she's used to him being scattered. "I'm Caroline," she tells Kyle. "I coach the women's soccer team, and we got in really late last night or I'd be more put together right now."

"I'm Kyle. We're having enchiladas for lunch, if you'd like to join us."

"Wow." Caroline glances at Aidan. "Someone's trying hard to make a good impression."

Aidan flushes. "I'm not the one in charge of cooking."

"There's soup too," Ritchie says.

Caroline looks closer at Aidan, before she gives Kyle the same scrutiny. She sighs as she curls an arm around Ritchie's shoulders. "Honey, were you actually invited for lunch or did you invite yourself?"

"I was invited," Ritchie answers, indignant, and he turns to Kyle for backup.

"I did invite him," Kyle says.

"See," Ritchie says. "He even wanted to hear about my garden."

"You told him about the garden?" Aidan asks. He rubs his forehead.

"You told me about the garden first," Kyle reminds him. "Besides, it's pretty cool. The apartment complex down the road from us is installing communal rooftop gardens."

"Will you move?" Aidan asks.

Kyle shuts his computer, because it's obvious he won't do any more work for a while. "Nah, I like my apartment. And Jenny and Charlotte wouldn't move for a garden."

"Jenny and Charlotte are your sisters?" Caroline asks.

"Best friends."

"Huh." Caroline looks between Aidan and Kyle again as if she's trying to puzzle them out. "Are you sure you're okay having company for lunch?"

Kyle lets Aidan field this one. This is his house, and these are his friends. Kyle's the interloper here, and he wrinkles his nose at the thought. It's one that doesn't sit right with him. He wishes he'd left that hickey on Aidan's neck after all.

"You're both welcome," Aidan says. "You can tell me about last night's game. How'd your team do?"

THEY EAT LUNCH together, and Ritchie probably would've stayed longer, but Caroline took one last look between the two of them and dragged Ritchie away.

"They seem nice," Kyle says once the door is shut, leaving Aidan and Kyle alone again. But now that they've been interrupted by lunch and Aidan's neighbors, Kyle isn't ready to jump back into make-outs. He has questions, ones they didn't need to answer when they went out with Charlotte and Jenny, because they've known from the beginning who Aidan is to Kyle. But maybe Aidan isn't as open with his friends as Kyle is with his.

"They've been dating longer than I've known them," Aidan says, moving into the living room. He brings his schoolwork with him, spreading it out across the coffee table which means Kyle isn't the only one feeling as though they've lost their moment.

Kyle drops onto the armchair with his e-reader.

"I don't think Ritchie realizes how long they've been together," Aidan continues. "I'm pretty sure Caroline's going to be the one who proposes or else it'll never happen."

"He seems scattered."

"That's the nice way to put it. I've shown him how to set reminders in his phone, but it doesn't help if he can't find his phone." Aidan shrugs.

"Caroline doesn't know what to make of us. She'll probably ambush you as soon as I'm gone."

"What do you want me to tell her?"

Kyle shrugs, as if this hasn't been buzzing around his brain for the past hour. "What does she already know?"

"She knows I date men," Aidan says.

"Ritchie too?" Kyle asks. "Next time he comes over, can I tell him we're getting ready for round two?"

"That'll probably go over his head," Aidan says. "I'll just lock the adjoining door next time."

"You could hang a tie on the door handle. That's a classic, right?"

"I can think of much better uses for my ties."

Kyle sets his e-reader aside. "Yeah? Want me to come over there and we can brainstorm?"

Aidan pushes the table away from the couch which is all the invitation Kyle needs. He abandons his chair for Aidan's lap, and Aidan spreads his legs, just enough to make it a stretch for Kyle to straddle them.

It isn't the most comfortable position, and Aidan smiles as if he knows that but wants it this way anyway.

"Making me work for you?" Kyle asks.

Aidan's smile grows.

"Or maybe—" Kyle slides forward until they're hip to hip "—this is what you wanted." Their chests are pressed together now, and Kyle whispers his words against Aidan's cheek, because there isn't enough space between them to be face to face.

Well, there'd be enough space if they were kissing, if Kyle tilted his head to fit their mouths together, but as much as he enjoys kissing Aidan, he wants to hold off, tease himself a little bit. He wants to see how far he can push before Aidan will take control.

He picks up where he left off earlier in the kitchen, kissing a path up the line of Aidan's jaw until he's at Aidan's ear and can nip at his earlobe. Aidan gasps, takes a sharp inhale of a breath, and digs his fingers into Kyle's hips. Maybe it's a warning, but it could just as easily be encouragement.

Kyle grins and bites harder, tugging this time, and Aidan grinds his hips into Kyle's, as if he needs something nice to counter the sharp sting of Kyle's teeth. Kyle works a hand between them so he can press his palm against the hardening line of Aidan's dick. The next time he bites, Aidan's dick jerks in his pants then grows harder, pressing up into Kyle's touch.

Kyle wants to bite somewhere he can leave a mark, somewhere he doesn't have to be as gentle. He grabs the hem of Aidan's shirt in his hands, determined to pull it off, but Aidan kisses him first, a bruising, desperate press of his lips.

And it's good, kissing is always good in Kyle's book, but he wants Aidan's shirt off. *Then* they can kiss. He turns his head, breaking the kiss, and he's breathing heavily as he pushes Aidan's shirt up a couple of inches.

It's as far as he gets before Aidan's mouth is on his again, one of Aidan's hands wrapped around the back of Kyle's neck to hold him there.

It's Kyle's turn to groan as Aidan's fingers dig into his skin, not hard enough to bruise, but enough for him to feel held. *Wanted.* Kyle drops a kiss against the corner of Aidan's mouth. He keeps his kisses gentle as he peppers them down Aidan's jaw, a contrast to the need that pounds alongside the beat of his heart.

It's a game of patience now, and Kyle's is nearly at its end, but he thinks, for the first time, he might finally have the upper hand on Aidan.

Kyle's lips barely brush Aidan's cheek when Aidan threads his fingers through Kyle's hair and pulls, hard enough that Kyle tips his head back, mouth parted on a gasp.

"I thought we were going to talk about ties," Aidan says.

"Talk is overrated."

Aidan laughs and loosens his hold on Kyle's hair. "You don't have anything to say? This must be a first."

"Maybe you should take over," Kyle says. "My mouth's about to be busy."

"Oh?"

Kyle grins and slides to his knees. Before Aidan can do anything more than say, "Oh," again, Kyle has his shirt shoved up, and he's finally leaving the mark he wants.

He sucks and nips at the skin stretched across Aidan's hipbone, not pulling off even when Aidan fists a hand in his hair and tugs. Kyle moans and tugs against the hold to make pain light up along his scalp. It feels good, and he bites harder against Aidan's skin.

"Maybe I'll use one of my ties on your mouth."

Kyle hums, bored. That's both unoriginal *and* counterproductive.

Aidan pulls on Kyle's hair, hard enough for tears to spring into his eyes, and Kyle reluctantly takes a break from the bruise he's leaving on Aidan's skin.

"It'd keep your mouth open," Aidan says, dragging his thumb against Kyle's bottom lip as if he's thinking about it, "but you wouldn't be able to say anything."

Kyle dips his head to take Aidan's thumb in his mouth.

"You wouldn't be able to do that either," Aidan says. "Maybe I'd trace my cock over your lips just to hear you whine."

Kyle whines now, thinking about it, and a flush blooms across his cheeks. He lets Aidan's thumb slip out of his mouth so he can rub his cheek against it. It leaves a smear of saliva against his skin, and Aidan's gaze is dark, *wanting*, as Kyle meets it.

Emboldened, Kyle slides his hands up Aidan's thighs until he reaches his waistband. They don't need to wait for what Aidan was talking about. They don't even need a tie. If Aidan wants Kyle desperate and begging for his cock, then he's more than happy to oblige.

As soon as Kyle hooks his fingers through Aidan's waistband, Aidan's hands shoot out to grab his bare wrists. There's nothing playful about the hold.

Kyle immediately stills, wondering what he's done wrong. When he looks up, Aidan shakes his head.

"I'm sorry," Aidan says. "This isn't—we're having a recovery day." He traces his fingers over the skin of Kyle's wrists and—

Oh. They didn't need Kyle's cuffs at the club so he left them at home, and he hadn't brought them here, and now; well, he supposes it doesn't matter. Aidan doesn't want this, and even though Kyle does, he drops his hands to his lap, away from temptation.

"We got carried away," Kyle says. "That's on both of us."

"This is probably a bad time to talk about last night."

"Probably." Kyle's still on his knees which is sometimes grounding for him, but right now it's sending too many conflicting signals to his brain. "How about we watch some TV until dinner and tackle talking afterward?"

At Aidan's nod, Kyle pushes to his feet.

"I'm just gonna—" Kyle jerks his thumb toward the bathroom. "If that's okay."

"Of course, it is. You're in charge of you right now."

Right, Kyle thinks. He has to resist the urge to rub his wrists as he heads down the hall to find the bathroom. By the time he's splashed some water on his face, disappointment and concern have killed his hard-on. *Well, that takes care of that, then.*

He washes his face once more for good measure and heads back into the living room. Aidan already has the TV on, but he's watching the local news which, "No," Kyle says, snatching the remote. He flips channels until he finds an *NCIS* marathon, because there's always one of those on. "You want to grade?"

"Not really." Aidan holds his arm up, an invitation to Kyle to sit next to him.

Kyle's quick to take it, plastering himself to Aidan's side. He understands why they're not doing anything right now. They've set down rules for a reason and even something light today after Kyle went so deep last night is pushing it for this early in a relationship. But still, rejection stings no matter how many good reasons there are for it, and Kyle's grateful for the contact as he burrows closer.

"You weren't gone very long," Aidan says as he curls his arm around Kyle's shoulders.

"I wasn't."

"Okay."

They let the conversation drop and settle in to watch the NCIS team solve a murder.

AFTER THEY'VE EATEN dinner and the leftovers are put away in the fridge for Aidan to take to work during the week, Kyle says, "Time to talk?"

Aidan nods and by mutual, unspoken agreement, they sit back down at the card table which serves as a dining room table. The island is for work, the couch is for softer things, and in Kyle's head, the table seems like a good place for serious conversations.

"You went deep last night," Aidan says, no hint of what he's thinking in his voice.

"I didn't expect to, but I wanted to. It's been a while, and I trust you."

"Do you know what caused it?"

"From the moment you opened the door, I knew you were in control, and last night, it really worked for me. I don't always like being micromanaged, but every time you gave me an order, every time I could turn over another decision to you, it was something I could let go of until I didn't even have to think at all. I could just *be*. I don't—" Kyle rubs the back of his neck. "I don't do it very often."

"Because you don't like it?"

Kyle takes a moment to sift through his thoughts, because there's a shadow of guilt on Aidan's face, and he doesn't want to make it worse. "Sometimes I don't want it, but sometimes I do. Like I said, last night it worked. But I get...pliant? And sometimes I don't like being that passive."

Kyle shrugs because if he doesn't, then he'll bunch his shoulders and curl in on himself while he waits for Aidan's reaction. He's been with people who were offended when he didn't drop for them every time, as if whether he floated in subspace or not was a measure of how good a Dom they were.

He's vulnerable when he lets himself go deep, and he doesn't trust just anyone with himself when he's there. It says something he's not sure he's ready to face about how easily he went down for Aidan the other night.

"I'm honored you trusted yourself to me," Aidan says, and it should sound old-fashioned, maybe even silly, but a warm flush spreads over Kyle's face. "I enjoyed it, but I've enjoyed our other scenes as well. I don't want you to feel obligated to go that deep every scene."

"Good, because I probably won't. Sometimes it feels really good, and sometimes I want to push to see how you'll push back."

Aidan's lips quirk up in a smile. "I've noticed. And that's something I wouldn't want to erase from our scenes. I like the challenge."

"I've gotta keep you on your toes," Kyle says. "Is this where we talk about our next scene?"

"Do you have some ideas?"

"I have a whole list. Not an actual list, but I could do that. Then we can cross off things we've tried."

"I could make an Excel sheet, so we can rate things. One for *don't do again* and five for *definitely do again.*"

"Spreadsheets?" Kyle shoots Aidan a look from under his eyelashes. "I'd rather you spread me over your sheets."

Aidan pushes Kyle out of his chair and laughs at his look of outrage.

Chapter Eight

JENNY BOOKS TIME in the studio on a Wednesday morning. At first, she'd joked about doing it early enough that Kyle would need to set three alarms and buy a coffee on the way, but she'd gone with a late-morning time slot after Kyle told her he wanted Aidan to be out of class when they're done.

Kyle's meeting Aidan at his house after the shoot, which will make this the first time he's gone anywhere but his own bedroom after a photoshoot with Jenny. Honestly, he would've been fine doing this earlier and hanging out at his apartment or even lounging around Aidan's house while he waited for him to come home from work, but Aidan's nervous about the shoot.

He offered to pick Kyle up from the studio, which was sweet, but completely unnecessary. Kyle's never done anything with Jenny that might compromise his ability to drive.

Kyle shows up to the studio in a pair of flannel pajama pants and a grey T-shirt, and he texts Aidan one last time before he tucks his phone away.

KYLE: *Don't forget to put a tie on the door when you get home :)*

Kyle grins, pleased with himself, as he saunters over to where Jenny's setting up the various screens and lights for the shoot.

"I don't want to know why you're smiling like that," she says.

"I have a hot date when this is over."

"Ugh," Jenny says but she's smiling, happy for him. "Speaking of hot, undress and tell me if I need to turn the heat up."

Kyle pulls his shirt over his head and pretends to think. "How perky do you want my nipples?"

"I'm already regretting this."

"Please, I'm your favorite model."

Kyle tugs his pants off and drops them on the floor with his shirt.

"Underwear?" Jenny asks when she sees his briefs. "Look at you being an actual adult."

"Just trying to impress you." Kyle wanders over to the wall jack, phone in hand.

"Nothing too loud," Jenny warns as he plugs in. "You know I can't concentrate with that screaming stuff."

"*That screaming stuff* is for workouts. I'm picking something with words so I don't fall asleep. None of this classical crap."

"It's soothing."

Kyle rolls his eyes and puts Pandora on so the internet can be blamed when neither of them like the song. He wanders back over to the set and runs a hand over the sturdy set of beams, vertical and horizontal. They form a frame, and Kyle tries to shake it to see if it moves.

"It'll hold you," Jenny promises.

"Suspension?" Kyle asks.

"Just for a couple of shots. I'm thinking a web motif."

"And I'm the poor unsuspecting fly who ends up trapped?"

"You're annoying enough to be a fly." Jenny flashes him a grin. "But you're too smart to make your way unknowingly into a web. You want to be there."

"You ever notice that art concepts are really fucking weird?"

"Is that my profession you're knocking? Remember, I'm the one tying you up. You should be nicer to me."

"Threats in the workplace? I'm so proud of you."

"Help me set up the web."

Jenny pulls out a silver rope, which is pretty enough to look at, but it's rougher than he likes to be tied with. There are eyehooks screwed into the wooden frame, and Jenny ties her end of the rope around one of them and begins to weave. Kyle's participation is limited to fetching more rope when Jenny needs it, but in the end, there's an unmistakable spider web created.

"All right," Jenny says. "Now, it's your turn. This will look really good."

Kyle eyes the spider web, dubious, but he doesn't hesitate to take his briefs off or go where Jenny directs him. Jenny is gentle with him, winding new rope, something softer this time, with practiced hands.

She only talks to him when she wants to check that something isn't too tight or that she isn't pulling his limbs at odd angles, which lets Kyle sink into a quiet place in his head. He doesn't have to worry about anything, because Jenny's taking care of him.

It's different than when they demo together, because Jenny will leave his side to take pictures, and she'll move him into different positions, but it's still good.

By the time they're done, Kyle's head is as quiet as it's been all week, and he smiles at her while he stretches his limbs out. "This was good. Thanks."

"Thank *you*," Jenny says. "I think we'll get a few good shots out of this."

"What's it for? Your website?"

"And an art show and the Bondage Expo."

"Busy, busy," Kyle says.

Jenny grins. "You know me. I was going to see if you wanted to be a live model for the Expo, but it sounds like that might not work."

"When is it?" Kyle's modeled for her at the Expo before, and he wouldn't mind doing it again.

"June."

Kyle switches to stretching his hamstrings. "That's pretty far away," he says. "I wouldn't write me off already."

"And you shouldn't write you off already. I thought things were good with Aidan."

"They are, but June's a way off, and I'm trying not to get too far ahead of myself." Kyle doesn't want to talk about this right now, though, because it's too soon for him to poison his pleasant headspace. "Will you give me copies of the pictures?"

"Of course. I know how vain you are."

Kyle grins and doesn't deny it.

He hangs out for a bit, has a bottle of water, has a snack, and he helps Jenny break down the set. He's back in his briefs now but nothing else because he didn't want to put the rest of his clothes on quite yet. It's a surefire signal to his brain that this is over, and he wants to cling to the serenity as long as he can.

A glance at his phone shows him he has a couple of messages waiting for him.

AIDAN: *Told you, I have better uses for my ties. I locked the door.*

AIDAN: *Not the front door, you can come in through there. You don't need to knock.*

Kyle grins and tells Aidan he's on his way. It's worth putting his clothes back on if it means seeing Aidan. Plus, if Kyle plays his cards right then he can probably lose them pretty quickly again.

"Ditching me?" Jenny guesses.

"I helped you clean up," Kyle says. "Besides, you have a lovely woman waiting for you at home. And I have an equally lovely man."

Jenny swats him on the ass and sends him on his way.

He uses his GPS to get to Aidan's house, not quite comfortable driving there without it yet. He parks behind Aidan's car and grabs his backpack out of the front seat, and by then Aidan already has the front door open.

"The real reason I don't need to knock," Kyle says. "Have you been lurking there since I texted you?"

Aidan shrugs, good as an admittance, but Kyle kind of likes the thought of Aidan hovering by the door and looking out the window every time he heard a car drive by until he saw Kyle's pull into the driveway.

Okay, Kyle *really* likes the thought, and he leans in to kiss Aidan right there on the front step. He wraps one arm around Aidan's waist and drops his overnight bag so he can fist the other hand in Aidan's shirt.

They kiss until Aidan pulls back, his expression dazed as he says, "We're in the doorway."

"Uh-huh," Kyle agrees, but he lets Aidan step back into the house. He grabs his bag off the step and follows Aidan in, shutting the door behind him and turning the lock. "Any objections now?"

"You're wearing too many clothes."

Kyle grins and tugs at the waistband of his pants so he can flash a bit of skin. "Says the man who refuses to get naked. But I can definitely do less clothes. Where do you want me?"

"Bedroom. I'll meet you there."

Kyle pulls Aidan in for a lingering kiss, one to hold him over, before heading to the bedroom. With no one here to impress, he doesn't bother taking his time. He strips out of his clothes quickly and shoves them into his bag after he pulls his cuffs out. The bag he kicks out of the way, but his cuffs are placed carefully on the bed.

He's shamelessly poking through Aidan's bedside drawer when Aidan comes in.

"It's a partial collection," Aidan says. "Most of it's in my closet."

"But people keep their favorites within reach, and a man's sex toys can tell you a lot about him."

Aidan shuts his drawer. "We don't need any of those right now."

"Gonna do all the work yourself?" Kyle asks. He spreads his legs and tugs on Aidan's hand until he's standing between them.

Aidan's gaze dips to Kyle's chest then his arms then his thighs, all the places where there are still faint marks from Jenny's rope, the kind of marks which'll fade within the hour, but there's the smallest wrinkle in Aidan's forehead as he takes them all in.

He looks like he wants to say something, but he keeps his mouth shut, and Kyle will figure out what he's thinking later. Right now, he offers his right wrist for Aidan to hold in his hands. With his left hand, Kyle holds out his first cuff.

"Will you?" Kyle asks.

Aidan's thumb brushes the small indents the rope left against Kyle's wrist and he takes the cuff and covers the marks with black leather. Something in his face relaxes once the cuff is hiding the marks, maybe because he can't see the evidence of the photoshoot anymore, or maybe because he can see the evidence that Kyle is *his*.

Kyle holds his second wrist out, and he'd be embarrassed at how his arm trembles in Aidan's hold, except Aidan smiles at him, soft, like this means as much to him as it does to Kyle. This is something he can't have with Jenny. She can wrap him with rope, make him look pretty, make him feel safe, but she can't make him feel *cherished*. Aidan looks at Kyle as if he's the most important thing in the room, and Kyle wants to bask in the attention, and he wants to return it.

He hooks his fingers through Aidan's belt loops and tugs him closer. When he tilts his head back, Aidan obliges him with a kiss, bending down to meet him. Kyle wraps his legs around Aidan's to keep him here and slips his hands under Aidan's shirt, because he's wearing entirely too many clothes.

Predictably, that's what makes Aidan pull back. "I want to focus on you right now."

"You can do that while shirtless." Kyle would also like him to take his pants off, but clearly he needs to take this one tiny step at a time.

"I can't give you everything you want," Aidan says, trailing a hand down Kyle's cheek. "I'll spoil you."

"Maybe I want to be spoiled," Kyle grumbles.

Aidan dips in for another kiss, and Kyle's made no secret of how much he loves kissing, which makes it hard to hold on to his irritation as Aidan *does* spoil him, kissing him deep and a little dirty, until Kyle has to break away to breathe.

Aidan pushes at Kyle's hips to move him toward the center of the bed and Kyle goes until he's flat on his back. He's rewarded with another kiss, and Aidan holds himself up over Kyle. It isn't close enough. Kyle wraps his arms around Aidan's shoulders and hooks a leg around Aidan's until he can pull him down onto Kyle's body.

Aidan's shirt rubs against his skin, soft enough to be a tease compared to the rough drag of denim against Kyle's thighs. Kyle wouldn't mind having red splotches from Aidan's jeans, but the rub of denim against his cock doesn't hurt in the right way to feel good.

"Will you take your pants off at least?" Kyle asks.

"You're the one being impatient. I have a plan."

Knowing Aidan, this plan involves him keeping all his clothes on. "What's step one?"

Aidan kneels up and there's a smile on his face when he touches Kyle's pecs, his thighs, all the places that are pink from rubbing against Aidan's clothes. "Step one is for you to turn over."

"Sounds like a bad plan," Kyle says, and Aidan brings the flat of his hand down on Kyle's thigh. It makes a cracking sound, louder than it is painful, and Kyle huffs before he turns on his stomach. "Better?"

"Better."

Kyle feels the dip of the bed as Aidan moves then the press of Aidan's knees as he straddles Kyle's thighs. What does Aidan hope to do from there? Kyle can't spread his legs enough for Aidan to fuck him, and there isn't a good angle for them to kiss. So far, he isn't interested in this plan at all.

"Relax," Aidan says, close enough that Kyle can feel the puff of his breath against the back of his neck.

"Make me," Kyle challenges.

Aidan curls one of his hands around Kyle's hip, but the other snakes around to settle on the vulnerable line of Kyle's throat. Aidan's touch isn't even firm, he's too careful to press hard, but Kyle's breath still hitches in his throat, and it feels as if Aidan catches it in his hand.

There's a moment where time seems frozen, Kyle's entire body on high alert, straining toward something he knows he shouldn't want, but then between one heartbeat and another, the world comes crashing back into him. His pulse thuds against Aidan's hand, muted and too loud at the same time.

His head is spinning and his breath comes too fast until Aidan's fingers press into his skin, holding him, and everything settles.

"Relax," Aidan says again.

This time, Kyle relaxes, body melting into the bed. He feels safe beneath Aidan, secure with Aidan's hands on him. He wants Aidan to press harder, but that's something they probably have to talk about first.

He wishes they were facing each other, wishes he could see what Aidan's gaze looks like right now, if he's as desperate for Kyle right now as Kyle is for him.

Maybe it's for the best they're not facing each other. Kyle would beg, lips parted, eyes hooded, and he'd press his throat into Aidan's hand until he gave Kyle what he wanted or had to back away.

Aidan shifts his hand from Kyle's neck to his shoulder, and Kyle's disappointed, but he doesn't move from where Aidan's put him.

Aidan rewards him with a kiss to his left shoulder then his right one. He kisses lower and lower still, and Kyle blames the fuzz in his brain for how long it takes him to realize Aidan's kissing the indents left from the rope. He's laying kisses against Kyle's skin, as if he's claiming it for himself.

"I didn't get hard when Jenny tied me up," Kyle says, playing a hunch. If Aidan wanted him quiet then he should've gagged him. Aidan pauses, breath hot against Kyle's skin, but he doesn't kiss him again.

"I never do," Kyle continues. "I always wait until later."

When the next kiss comes, the touch of Aidan's lips is even briefer than the previous ones. Aidan's too controlled, too put together. Kyle wants him as desperate as he is, and he knows how to do it. He just doesn't know what'll happen once he gets Aidan there.

"Jenny took a lot of pictures," Kyle says, stretching out to call attention to all the fading marks on his skin. "Pictures of me naked, bound in rope and displayed to look my best. She's putting the pictures on her website for anyone to look at. They'll probably be in her next book too. Who only knows how many people will see them. Will see *me*."

Aidan presses his fingers against Kyle's hips, his nails digging into Kyle's skin hard enough to leave marks of his own, before he forces himself to relax.

Kyle wants more.

"That's what I always jerk off to afterwards," Kyle says. "After I've gone home, I wrap my hand around my dick and think about how many people will see me."

Kyle reaches a hand down so Aidan will smack it away with a sharp, "No," that makes him groan and grind against the mattress. He wants Aidan to be rough with him, wants bruises that will last all week. He wants Aidan to hold him, own him, control him, but with an edge they didn't have last Friday night.

"I always come so hard after a photoshoot. I think about all the people who will see pictures of me and think about how they'll jerk off to me, whether they'll rub one out over their shorts or if they'll take the time to at least shove their waistband down."

Aidan growls against Kyle's skin, and Kyle shudders because this is closer to what he wants.

"And I looked good. Jenny brought lavender rope just for me, because she knows how good it looks against my skin. You can see some of the places where she wound the rope around me. It held me tight, didn't it?"

Aidan drops his forehead to the small of Kyle's back. He's breathing hard, but Kyle can feel, and hear, as he brings it back under control. This is the opposite of what Kyle hoped for, and maybe he's going about this the wrong way. Maybe he should try asking for what he wants.

Kyle turns over, almost hitting Aidan in the head, but Aidan moves back just in time. Before Aidan can say something, scold him for changing position, Kyle grabs Aidan's hands and puts them on his stomach where there are still faint imprints from the rope.

"Hold me tighter," Kyle challenges. "Leave marks that'll last longer."

He wants Aidan's nails digging into his skin and Aidan's teeth leaving sharp, stinging marks. He wants to wake up tomorrow with bruises and hickeys. He wants to wake up feeling owned.

"Fuck," Kyle says. He needs to touch his cock. He needs friction, *something* before he goes out of his mind.

His fingers only graze his cock for a moment before Aidan pins his wrists to the bed.

"I told you no," Aidan reminds him. "Do I need to remove the temptation?"

Kyle nods. There are some days his self-control is good enough to hold back on his own, but today isn't one of those days.

Aidan opens his nightstand drawer and pulls out a clip. "Hands above your head."

Kyle obediently lifts his arms and watches the best he can as Aidan clips his cuffs together around one of the slats in the headboard. It means Kyle can't bring his arms back down, can't touch himself. He won't get anything except what Aidan gives him, and the thought makes him squirm.

"You won't get free," Aidan tells him.

"I don't want to. I want you to touch me."

"I thought you wanted more than that," Aidan says. He moves back down Kyle's body, until he's straddling his knees so that when he bends down, it's easy for his teeth to latch on to the thin skin covering Kyle's hipbone.

"Oh," Kyle says as Aidan sucks a mark there. His hips shift restlessly, and his cock bobs because Aidan's mouth is *right there* but Aidan doesn't pay any attention to it.

When Aidan pulls back to look at his handiwork, the skin is already pink, and it feels tender, prickly, like Kyle can feel the blood rising to the surface. Aidan waits until he has Kyle's full attention to press his thumb against the mark, and Kyle writhes, trying to push into the touch and move away from it.

"Is this what you want?" Aidan asks.

"*Yes.*" Kyle tugs on his restraints to feel his cuffs against his wrists, and he pushes his hips up into Aidan's hand to feel the mark against his skin. "More. Please. I want to be covered."

"Greedy," Aidan says, and even though he utters the word like a compliment, Kyle flushes. He nods too, and Aidan grins at him, all teeth, before he picks his next spot to mark.

Aidan isn't gentle, but Kyle doesn't want him to be. Kyle groans and rolls his hips against empty air every time Aidan catches a bit of skin between his teeth and bites. He gasps every time Aidan sucks against a growing mark, and tears spring into his eyes when Aidan ducks down to work his way up his inner thighs, careful he doesn't touch Kyle's cock when he moves.

"Something wrong?" Aidan asks, looking up from between Kyle's legs. Kyle's cock spurts out more precome and Aidan smiles, nothing friendly about it. "Isn't this what you wanted?"

"Touch my cock. Please."

"No," Aidan says, and somehow Kyle's dick gets even harder. "You can keep begging, though, I like it."

Kyle drops his head back against the pillows. "Please. Touch me."

"I am." Aidan dips his head down to suck a bruise against Kyle's inner thigh.

"More," Kyle says.

When Aidan's teeth nip at already sensitive skin, Kyle's hips buck up, and Aidan holds him down with a forearm across his stomach. Kyle curls his hands into fists, because he needs to hold on to something, but his hands close around empty air.

Even with Aidan pinning him to the bed, he feels like he's about to float away, desperate and needing and close, but not close enough.

"Please," he says again.

He continues to plead as Aidan leaves marks across Kyle's thighs and stomach, always careful not to touch Kyle's cock. When Aidan finally leans back on his heels, his lips are a dark red and there's a hint of pride in his eyes as he looks over the marks he's made.

There are dozens of them, and Kyle knows he's flushed, and his hair is a wreck from tossing his head back and forth. His cock is throbbing, and there's precome splattered across his stomach and tears in his eyes, and Aidan's still in all his fucking clothes.

"Please," Kyle says, almost a whisper, his voice raspy from overuse.

Aidan isn't touching him at all anymore, and Kyle needs even a hand against his ankle. *Aidan took the time to mark me. He won't leave me. I'm his. That's what all these bruises mean.*

Aidan smiles, the gentlest expression he's had on his face since Kyle showed up at his house. He unclips Kyle's cuffs and sits back as Kyle drops his hands to his sides. He's not quite brave enough to try and touch Aidan. He doesn't want to be told no again. Earlier, it was good; it wound him up, but now he's too needy to play games.

"Touch yourself," Aidan says. "That's what you do after photoshoots, right?"

Kyle nods and wraps a hand around his dick. He's been steadily leaking precome which means his hand doesn't drag painfully against his dick, but it isn't as slick as he likes.

"This is a little different than usual," Kyle says. He drops his free hand to his hip so he can press his fingers against the first bruise Aidan left. Pain sparks beneath his skin, and he squeezes his cock, because it's the exact right kind of pain.

"Usually I think about all the people who'll be looking at me, but today I'm only thinking about you."

Aidan pushes Kyle's legs further apart, baring him for his gaze. "Tell me."

"I'll carry your marks for days. I'll see them every time I shower, every time I change my clothes." Kyle's strokes lose their rhythm as he gets closer, thinking about how Aidan's teeth felt digging into his skin and how Kyle will try to recreate the moment by pressing his fingers against the same places.

"It's my hand that'll get me off, but it's you who'll get me hard," Kyle says. "Your mouth, your teeth, the way you put your claim on me." He pauses to drag in two much needed breaths. He stutters on his exhale but he doesn't stop talking. He can't, not now that he has Aidan's entire focus on him.

"Please," Kyle says. "Tell me I can come. I want to hear you say it. Give me permission. Please."

"Come," Aidan tells him. "For me. Look at me while you do it."

"Yes. Thank you. Th—" His words of gratitude are cut off by a moan when he finally comes, cock spurting into his fist, his gaze locked on Aidan.

He doesn't look away, not as his orgasm knocks through him, not as he falls against the bed again. Not even when he wipes his hand on his thighs.

"Your turn?" Kyle asks. "I want to see you come."

"You want everything," Aidan says.

"Yes." Kyle refuses to be ashamed of it. "This is something I don't get from a photoshoot. I can imagine how people are affected by me, but I can't see it. Show me what I do to you. Let me see how hard you are because you've been watching me. Let me see you come. Please."

It's Aidan's turn to suck in a sharp breath, and Kyle's hands move to Aidan's thighs, but he doesn't move his hands to Aidan's fly, doesn't take what he hasn't been given.

"You're different from them," Kyle continues. "You don't see me through a screen or on a piece of paper. You have me, right here, in front of you."

"I do." Aidan pops the button on his jeans. "Do you think you deserve to see me come?"

"Yes." Kyle props himself up on his elbows for a better view. "I've been good for you. I came here and put on a show only for you. I let you mark me up, let you claim me. Now, I want you to finish it. Come on me. *Please.* I want to rub your come into the marks you made until I feel owned."

"Keep talking," Aidan demands, as if Kyle was about to stop.

Aidan shoves his jeans and his boxers down enough to pull his cock out, and Kyle licks his lips. He'd give up talking if it meant he could suck Aidan's cock, but that's for another day.

"I'm here for *you*," Kyle says. As much as he was teasing earlier, this is the truth. "I'm in your bed because I want *you*. Everyone else, they can imagine me in their beds, but I'm in yours. Use me. Cover me in your come. Rub it in. You can because I'm yours. Please, I—"

Aidan comes with a grunt, striping his come across Kyle's stomach.

"Thank you," Kyle says. "Will you—?"

He doesn't finish before Aidan is rubbing his come into Kyle's skin. It mixes with Kyle's come and covers the marks Aidan's made and covers Kyle's unmarked skin too, and he knows it'll wash off in the shower, but right now, with Aidan's hands on him and Aidan's marks on him, Kyle feels owned. He feels *wanted*.

He shimmies, comfortable and happy and pleased with how this morning's gone.

"You're a mess," Aidan says.

"Yeah," Kyle says, smug, "because you made me this way."

Aidan groans and drops his head to Kyle's shoulder.

"We should do this again sometime," Kyle says. "Maybe come on my face next time. I look good with come clinging to my eyelashes."

"You're going to kill me."

"I hope not. I have a lot of plans for you. You can put this down as a five on your spreadsheet."

"I don't actually have a spreadsheet," Aidan says. He nuzzles closer when Kyle runs a hand through his hair. "We should shower."

"Not yet," Kyle says. "Kiss me for a bit first. Then we can shower, and maybe nap."

"Did I wear you out?"

Aidan tries to smirk, but the look is ruined when he has to cover a yawn.

Kyle laughs and ruffles his hair.

Chapter Nine

KYLE WAKES UP pleasantly sore in the morning. When he stretches out in bed, he grins at the marks that cover his body. Each one of them is a reminder of last night, of Aidan's fingers or teeth mapping out his body and claiming it.

He tugs his pajama pants down enough to see the dark bruises on his hip. He snaps a picture to send Aidan.

KYLE: *I have a good view this morning.*

He rolls out of bed and forgoes a shirt as he wanders into the kitchen to make breakfast. He eats then settles in front of his computer to work, still shirtless.

He logs into his computer and admires the finger-shaped bruises on his waist from where Aidan gripped him just right.

His computer loads and goes to sleep before he remembers he was doing work.

He logs back into his computer and opens up his Wanda folder, because there's something wrong about working on a project for a library fundraiser while he's sporting a semi. He looks over Wanda's suggestions for the next e-blast. She wants to advertise the bondage demo next week and the flogging demo the week after. He wishes he wasn't off the demo circuit. He wouldn't mind being put on display on the stage and letting someone work him over.

He grabs a piece of paper so he can sketch out his thoughts, and as he's reaching for his pencil, he sees the bite marks scattered down his sides.

He stares long enough for his computer to fall asleep again.

Focus, he orders himself.

The fourth time he catches himself tracing the marks Aidan left behind, he stands up. He checks the time to make sure Aidan isn't in class and tugs the waistband of his pajamas down. He takes a picture of his dick, half-hard, and texts, *maybe too good a view*, before he tracks down a shirt.

He pulls his shirt over his head then wonders if maybe he should do the opposite. Would a shower and a jerk-off session solve his distraction issues faster?

Kyle's phone pings as he lifts his shirt over his head.

AIDAN: *Is that for me?*

Kyle rolls his eyes.

KYLE: *You know it is.*

Who else would it be for? Kyle doesn't think about anyone else these days. His thoughts are full of the last time he was with Aidan and the next time he'll be with him and all the things he wants to do with Aidan when they're together.

AIDAN: *Then save it for me.*

Kyle groans and knocks his head against the wall. He should've just showered.

KYLE: *Will I see you tonight?*

AIDAN: *Yes. Club? Only for a bit, I have early classes tomorrow.*

Kyle can wait until tonight to get off. He doesn't especially want to, but he can. And Aidan always makes the wait worth it.

KYLE: *Okay. Going to take a much less pleasant shower than I had planned.*

He leaves his phone on his bed and takes a cool shower. When he's done, there are goose bumps up and down his arms, and he pulls on long pants and a long-sleeved shirt.

At least there's nothing to distract him now.

Except for what Aidan has in store for tonight.

He groans.

He brings his phone back into the kitchen with him so he can set a twenty minute timer. Looks like today will be a forced productivity day. Twenty minutes of work, five minutes off until he either falls into a groove or it's time for lunch.

KYLE WEARS A loose pair of jeans to Enchanting Encounters because he didn't feel like squeezing himself into his tight ones. He's tortured himself enough for one day. His T-shirt is white and see-through if he holds the fabric tight against his skin. He searched his drawer until he found one faded enough to suit his purposes.

He isn't obviously marked by Aidan, but anyone who looks close enough will be able to see what the two of them were up to last night.

Aidan certainly notices, his gaze raking over Kyle's shirt and lingering where he knows he left marks. Kyle grins and slinks close enough to slot a thigh between Aidan's legs.

"I guess I don't have to ask if you're happy to see me," Kyle says.

Aidan rolls his eyes even as a smile tugs at his lips. He slides a hand into Kyle's back pocket and turns them toward the bar. "What do you want to drink?"

"Beer. In a bottle." Kyle winks and flicks his tongue out to wet his lips.

"Should I be worried that you're trying to seduce me or that you're doing such a poor job of it?"

"Are you telling me I need to try harder?"

Aidan pauses in the middle of the room. "I'm telling you that you don't need to try at all. You already have me."

"Sweet." Kyle presses a quick kiss to Aidan before they continue to the bar.

TJ's behind the bar, only him because it's a Thursday night. It's quiet enough that he heads their way as soon as they lean against the bar. When Aidan orders two beers, TJ lifts his eyebrows.

"Work night," Aidan explains, "but he likes to be social so here we are."

Kyle turns to Aidan as soon as TJ's gone. It's his turn to arch his eyebrows. "You say *he likes to be social* but what I hear is *he's desperate for attention.*"

"I wouldn't say desperate." Aidan tucks his hand back into Kyle's pocket. "And you certainly flourish under attention."

"Then why didn't we stay in so I could flourish under yours?"

"It's good for us to get out," Aidan answers. "We saw each other last night. You should take tonight to talk to your friends here."

"I should, should I?"

"It would make me happy if you did."

He's not sure what kind of game they're playing, but he's willing to go along with it until he figures out what's going on. "Okay." When TJ returns with their beers, Kyle takes his and asks, "What are the rules?"

"When I'm ready to go, we leave." Aidan catches Kyle's gaze and holds it.

Kyle raises his beer to his lips and smirks as Aidan stares. "I think I can handle that."

Aidan wants to see him mingle and flirt and have a good time? It's a little weird, but Kyle can do that. Aidan slides his hand up until his palm presses against one of the bruises he left last night.

Oh. This is what he wants.

He wants to set Kyle loose then see him obey when he calls.

I can definitely work with this.

Kyle leans in to brush his lips over Aidan's cheek, a tease more than anything, then he slips away.

He finds Lou and Renee sitting in a booth together, and he slides in next to Renee.

"Well, look who's decided to grace us with his presence," Lou says.

Kyle grins and wraps his lips suggestively around his beer bottle.

"Shameless," Lou says but he laughs.

Lou's in a mesh shirt which means he's picking up tonight. To his right, Renee's in a pair of heeled boots, which makes Kyle wonder how much freedom he has tonight.

"Like what you see?" Renee asks. She taps one of her heels against Kyle's calves.

Her lips curve up into a wicked smile as he visibly swallows.

"Always," he tells her.

"Flirt."

"More like tease tonight." Kyle's been with Doms who've sent him out to have a little fun before returning to their side for the rest of the night, but Aidan's not like that. Kyle presses his fingers against one of the marks Aidan left behind last night. Kyle can flirt and have a little fun, but he's already claimed. He knows who he's going home with tonight.

"Is that how it is?" Renee asks. "Aidan wants to keep you all for himself?"

"Who wouldn't?"

Lou groans and looks at his Sprite as if he wishes there was alcohol in it.

"It's a shame," Renee says. "I wouldn't have minded putting you under the table."

"Yeah?"

Renee leans forward. "I can think of a few things for you to do while you're down there." She drags her thumb across his bottom lip. When his eyes slip close, she pulls back. "But since that's not on the agenda tonight, you can help us find someone for Lou."

"Sounds fun," Kyle says. He turns his attention to Lou. "What're you looking for tonight?"

Lou slides down in the booth as if he wishes they'd go back to flirting and ignoring him. "Something. I dunno. I've been restless the past few days."

Kyle's been in Lou's position enough times to know that feeling. "We'll find someone to knock that restlessness right out of you." He studies Lou's reaction—none—and says, "Or maybe not. Are you looking for someone to tell you what to do?"

"I don't know what I want. I want someone to tell me what I want."

It's not a lot to go off, but Kyle can try. At least it'll give him something to do while he waits for Aidan.

"Wait!" Lou calls, but Kyle's already gone.

He works the room, chatting with acquaintances and catching up with friends. When he spots Rachel talking to a few guys he doesn't know he heads their way. If Lou doesn't know what he wants, then maybe an unknown is exactly what he needs.

"Here comes trouble," Rachel says as Kyle slinks over to them.

"No trouble tonight," Kyle promises as the circle opens up for him. "I'm looking for Lou."

"Ah."

"Not yourself?" one of the guys asks. He gives Kyle a blatant once-over, which is flattering, but Kyle should make sure there aren't any misunderstandings.

"My dance card's all full up." Kyle glances over his shoulder at the bar. Aidan's still where Kyle left him. He's talking to Doyle, but he looks up, as if he can sense that Kyle's watching him.

"He seems relaxed," the guy says.

"Why wouldn't he be?" Kyle asks. "He knows he's the one I'm leaving with at the end of the night."

"Ugh," Rachel says. "You and your *feelings* and *commitment*."

"I finally found someone who appreciates how awesome I am."

"Awesome isn't the word I'd pick." Rachel tousles his hair. "Jordan's the one checking you out, Jacob's his sub, and that's Jamaal."

Jordan has his fingers hooked through the O-ring in Jacob's wrist cuff. Jacob has relaxed since finding out that Kyle's taken, and Kyle forgoes flirting with Jordan to eye Jamaal instead. He's on Kyle's left, tall enough to make Kyle feel short.

"So," Kyle says. He slides a hand into his pocket to tug his pants down a couple of inches. "Are you looking for something tonight?"

"You seem like a lot of work. And you just finished telling us you have someone."

"Yes, on both counts, but I'm asking for a friend." He offers Jamaal his brightest smile. "And I think you might be a good fit. Well—" Kyle's eyes drift down to Jamaal's crotch. "Maybe not. Guess your dick is proportional."

Rachel chokes on her laugh. "I'm sorry," she tells Jamaal. She smacks Kyle's shoulder. "Are you trying to make Lou look good in comparison?"

"He doesn't need the help." Lou might be boring sometimes, but he's Kyle's friend, and he deserves a fun night. "You want to meet him?" Kyle asks Jamaal.

Jamaal eyes Kyle, suspicious. "You say he's less work than you?"

"That's not saying much," Rachel interjects. "But he's a good sub. Not enough fight for my tastes, though."

"I don't want to fight," Jamaal says.

"A softie." Kyle's tempted to coo, but he doesn't want to ruin Lou's night. "Come on, buddy. I haven't seen you around before, so I'm going to cheerfully threaten you as we walk over."

"Do you ever shut up?" Jamaal asks as he follows Kyle across the floor.

"There are a few guaranteed ways to do it, but you don't seem interested in any of them." Kyle delivers Jamaal to the table with a flourish and an introduction.

Lou's slack-jawed as he stares, and Kyle grins, proud of himself.

"That's my cue to leave," Renee says. She slips out and hooks her arm through Kyle's.

Kyle's phone buzzes once they're a few feet from the table.

AIDAN: *Playing matchmaker?*

KYLE: *Have to entertain myself somehow. I already know who I'm going home with.*

"Where'd you find Jamaal?" Renee asks.

"He was with Rachel and two other guys I haven't seen before. Maybe she has friends visiting?"

"Hopefully it's a long visit." She glances back at the table they left behind. Lou's already on his knees, his head tilted up toward Jamaal as they talk. "Are you going to help me now?"

"You don't need my help," Kyle says.

His phone buzzes again.

AIDAN: *Time to go.*

Kyle's lips twitch up in a smile.

"You're about to ditch me," Renee says.

"Yup." He finishes his beer in one last swallow. "I saw Cynthia earlier. I'm sure she'll be up for something. She might even lick your boots if you ask nice enough."

"Mmm," Renee says. "I haven't done a good boot worship scene in a while. You *are* full of good ideas tonight."

"I'm about to be full of something else." Kyle laughs as Renee shoves him toward the bar.

He's still laughing as he sets his empty bottle on the bar and slings his arm around Aidan's waist. "No one loves me."

"You're dramatic tonight." Aidan pulls Kyle closer and they leave together.

"Are we going to your place because you have work tomorrow?" Kyle asks. He wouldn't mind spending tonight in his apartment, Aidan spread out on his sheets. Kyle has Aidan's marks scattered up and down his body, and now he wants Aidan in his home. He wants Aidan in his shower, using his towels, sleeping in Kyle's bed.

"You're going to your place," Aidan says, "and I'm going to mine."

Kyle stops in the middle of the parking lot. *This* isn't where he thought tonight was headed. Last night had been so good, and tonight had picked up where they left off, and now Aidan wants them in separate places? If his body wasn't covered in the evidence of how much Aidan wants him, he'd feel insecure.

"You'll call me when you're home, and you'll tell me everything we'd do if I did take you home."

"Or," Kyle counters. "You could actually take me home, and we could do all those things together."

"Next time. If you make a convincing enough argument."

"I hate you a little bit right now," Kyle says, but he lets Aidan herd him toward their cars.

"You'll hate me less when you're begging me to let you come," Aidan says, confident.

Kyle leans against his car and pulls Aidan in for a kiss, because one, Aidan's confidence is always hot, and two, Kyle isn't leaving tonight without *something*. It's been less than twenty-four hours since Aidan touched him, kissed him, and Kyle still feels desperate for it.

He's tried his best not to get carried away with everything he wants, but he can't help thinking about how nice it'll be when they spend the night and the whole next day at each other's places. Kyle will be able to take a kiss whenever he wants one, then. He won't have to hoard them like he does now.

He's already planning breakfast in a pair of Aidan's pajama pants, sees himself pushing eggs around a skillet while Aidan kisses Kyle's neck and shoulders. Kyle tucks his hands into Aidan's back pockets and pulls him closer.

It's still not close enough.

He spreads his legs to pull Aidan between them. "You can still change your mind." He grinds his hips against Aidan's so he can feel how hard Kyle is, how much he wants this. "We can go to your place. I won't even stay long, if you're worried I'll get in the way of your work routine."

Aidan pulls back which is the exact opposite of what Kyle wants, and he's frowning which means Kyle's said something wrong.

"Or we can kiss again. That's good too."

He leans in, telegraphing his intention, and he's disappointed when his lips meet Aidan's fingers instead of his mouth.

"You aren't a disruption," Aidan promises.

His two fingers are still pressed against Kyle's lips so Kyle's careful not to groan out loud. He's even careful to hold back his sigh so Aidan won't feel it. Kyle didn't mean to start a *talk*. He doesn't want to talk. He wants Aidan's hands in his hair and his lips pressed against Kyle's.

"You're not a burden or whatever you're thinking," Aidan continues. "Tomorrow, I'd like it if you were at my house when I come home from work. We can spend the weekend together; my place, your place, the club, anywhere we want to go. I'm not pushing you away."

Aidan finds the deepest bruise he made last night and covers it with his other hand. "You're mine, as long as you want to be."

Kyle knocks Aidan's fingers away from his mouth so he can kiss him. He bites at Aidan's lips, hooking his fingers through Aidan's belt loops and yanking him closer.

"You can't just say shit like that." Kyle flips them so he can pin Aidan against his car. He wants to mark and claim. He wants so much he's dizzy with it. Is this how Aidan feels all the time? When Kyle's stripped bare and laid out before him? Too much that he wants to even know where to start?

"I mean it," Aidan says. "Every word."

Kyle tucks his face against Aidan's neck. His heart feels as if it'll beat out of his chest. "I'll see you tomorrow?"

"And phone call tonight." Aidan wraps a strong arm around Kyle's waist, holding him up. "Unless it's too much."

He shakes his head. "You said I'm yours. I want you, any way you'll let me."

"Phone call, then. Are you good to drive?"

Kyle groans. "Yes. No speeding, no rolling stops. I'll even stop for yellow lights."

"And both hands on the wheel," Aidan says, a smile in his words.

Kyle nods. He takes a step back and leans in for another kiss. He knows the sooner he leaves, the sooner he'll have Aidan on the phone, but that means leaving.

"One more kiss and then we should go," Kyle says.

"Are you asking or telling me?"

"Both," Kyle says. "Mostly telling, so you'll be my self-control."

Aidan smiles, soft, his eyes crinkling. He pulls Kyle in for their gentlest kiss of the night. Kyle's eyes flutter shut as he leans into Aidan, letting him hold both of them up. There's none of their earlier urgency, no restlessness in Kyle that's searching for an outlet.

When they pull back, Kyle's lips tingle.

"Phone call," Kyle says. And tomorrow, they'll be together as much as Kyle wants them to be.

Chapter Ten

A SMALL THRILL passes through Kyle as he lets himself into Aidan's house. Aidan's still at work, so Kyle's car is the only one in the driveway, and it makes something flutter in his chest. Aidan trusts him enough to let Kyle wander through his house unsupervised.

It's maybe a silly thought, because Kyle trusts Aidan with his body, trusts him not to hurt him too much, trusts him enough to slip into subspace and watch over Kyle when he's not in a position to watch out for himself. In comparison, Aidan giving Kyle the keys to his house isn't as important.

Still, it feels like a big deal.

Kyle pokes around Aidan's kitchen first. He looks in all his cupboards, inventories the fridge then the pantry. He makes a mental grocery list as he drifts into the living room then wanders back into the bedroom.

He doesn't open drawers or look under Aidan's mattress or help himself to a tour of Aidan's closet, because he believes in some boundaries, but his eyes do catch on the half-full laundry basket.

He knows Aidan likes to shower when he comes home from work, and Kyle—Kyle has an idea.

Aidan keeps saying that him not getting naked isn't a *thing* so Kyle feels no qualms about pushing.

He takes the laundry basket into the bathroom and pulls every towel he can find from the closet—bath towels, hand towels, facecloths—and he drops them all in the laundry basket. He takes the towel hanging up on the back of the door and the hand towel on the counter.

He grabs the dishtowels for good measure and dumps them all in the washing machine. Before he can overthink—or maybe properly think—about what he's doing, he adds some detergent and turns the machine on.

Once the washer rumbles to life, he closes the doors to mute the sound, and returns to the kitchen to see if he can make anything edible out of what Aidan has in his house. Next time he'll plan in advance and bring groceries with him.

The chicken is still in the oven when Aidan comes home, front door hitting the wall as it swings open.

Kyle stirs the rice before going into the living room to say hi. He bites his tongue against a, "How was your day?" or, "Glad you're home"; anything that sounds too domestic. He can't help the smile that says all those things.

He watches as Aidan dumps his messenger bag on the coffee table and his backpack on the couch. Aidan's jacket is rumpled from his bags, and his hair is windblown and a mess. His cheeks are pink from the wind or the heat in his car, and Kyle *wants*.

Next time I'm here when Aidan comes home from work, I'll greet him with a blowjob.

Aidan runs a hand through his hair as he looks up. He startles when he sees Kyle as if he'd forgotten Kyle would be here.

"Surprise," Kyle says.

Aidan flushes. "I knew you'd be here. I just—" He waves a hand.

"It's Friday. Your students fried your brain. Dinner still has another thirty minutes if you want to shower or whatever. Don't let me mess with your routine."

"Having dinner made for me is definitely messing with my routine." Aidan shrugs out of his jacket and drops it on his backpack. "But I won't complain about it."

"I should hope not."

"I like the idea of adjusting my routine and figuring out where you fit into it."

"I have a few ideas of where I can fit later." Kyle waggles his eyebrows.

Aidan huffs out a laugh. "I'm sure you do. But shower first, then dinner."

Kyle nods and hopes he doesn't look too eager. Or, if he does, that Aidan assumes it has to do with tonight's plans.

Aidan passes Kyle on the way to the hallway, and he pauses to kiss Kyle's cheek. "Hi. I don't think I said that earlier."

"Kisses work just as well," Kyle promises. He presses a featherlight kiss against Aidan's lips. "More of this after your shower?"

"After dinner," Aidan corrects. "But definitely more later."

Kyle grins and steals one last kiss before he returns to the kitchen. He stirs the rice then pulls a bag of frozen vegetables out of the freezer. He'd prefer to do this with fresh vegetables, but he's a man who knows how to adapt.

He dumps the veggies into a pot of water and turns the burner on. He grins when he hears the shower turn on. Is Aidan the kind of man who wants to rinse off when he gets home? Or does he like a long, hot shower to soothe away a full week of work? Will he shower quicker than usual because he knows Kyle's out here waiting? Or will he take his time, because he knows Kyle's anticipation will grow with each minute that passes?

Dinner is finished and keeping warm in the oven when the shower turns off.

He's just finished setting the table when Aidan calls his name.

He grins as he heads down the hall. He makes a half-hearted attempt to look more contrite as he knocks on the bathroom door. He hasn't made much progress when he opens the door, revealing a wet, naked Aidan.

Kyle doesn't even pretend he isn't staring, starting with Aidan's bare feet then dragging his gaze up Aidan's legs, his soft dick, his stomach, his chest, his shoulders, all the way up to his face.

"Really?" Aidan asks.

Kyle isn't done looking. He's not sure he ever could be. He doesn't understand why Aidan's been hiding from him. He doesn't have the body of someone who goes to the gym every morning, he's soft around the middle, and his muscles aren't as defined as Kyle's, but he shouldn't be ashamed of himself. Kyle likes him. A lot, actually.

"I'm admiring the view," Kyle says. "It's a new one."

"All my towels are missing," Aidan says as he drips onto the bathmat.

"Oh." Kyle aims for apologetic, but he isn't that good an actor. "I had some free time so I thought I'd run a load of laundry."

The washing machine chooses this moment to helpfully beep the end of its cycle.

"Uh-huh." Aidan looks a mixture of incredulous and amused. "And all my towels happened to be dirty?"

"I wasn't sure," Kyle answers. "Figured I'd be on the safe side."

"Will dinner keep?"

Kyle stops watching droplets of water run down Aidan's chest as his gaze snaps to Aidan's. Kyle's tongue darts out to wet his lips. "Yeah. I can throw it all in a casserole dish and we can heat it up later."

Did his plan work? Will he have Aidan naked before dinner and after it too?

"Do that," Aidan says, "then get your cuffs and meet me in my bedroom."

There's something firm to the order; Aidan doesn't sound angry, but Kyle knows there'll be some kind of punishment involved. He knew it would happen, and he can't help but look forward to what Aidan will come up with.

"Any way I can convince you to leave the bathroom first?" Kyle asks, because if he's already pushed this much he might as well go all the way.

Aidan's lips twitch as if he's trying not to smile. "Go."

Kyle goes.

He switches the laundry from the washer to the dryer, because at some point tonight, they'll probably want towels. He puts dinner in a casserole dish then does the dishes so they aren't sitting out for the next hour. Once the kitchen is clean and he's double-checked to make sure all the burners are off, Kyle heads into Aidan's bedroom.

Aidan's drying himself off with a beach towel. "Guess you missed a few."

"I was doing you a favor," Kyle reminds him. "Why would your beach towels be dirty? It's not summer anymore."

"Right. You were doing *me* a favor." Aidan runs his towel through his hair one last time before he drops it where his laundry basket would be if it wasn't out by the washing machine.

"Put your cuffs on the bed then strip," Aidan orders.

Kyle takes his cuffs out of his bag, then sets them gently on the bed. He's rougher with his clothes. He yanks his shirt off and shoves his pants down. He tosses them to the side. He doesn't bother putting on a show, too focused on the end goal. He and Aidan are about to be naked together for the first time. Kyle's about to get *something*, even though he's not sure what that something will be.

He wants to find out, though, and the sooner he listens, the sooner he'll be rewarded.

"Kneel on the bed," Aidan says.

Kyle kneels.

Aidan walks over, just out of reach even though Kyle wouldn't try to touch without permission. He's already pushed enough and, as he follows more orders, he slips into a different headspace. He doesn't need to push, because Aidan's here, and he'll give Kyle what he needs.

"Hand me your first cuff."

Kyle's stomach flips with anticipation and excitement as he holds out his first cuff. He offers up his right wrist without being asked. Aidan brushes his thumb over the thin skin covering his pulse as a reward.

He doesn't feel settled when his first cuff is buckled, too many things he wants, too many possibilities unfolding in his mind, but all the noise quiets as Aidan buckles the second. Whatever Kyle's done up to this point to start tonight, he's about to see what will come of it.

Aidan curls his fingers around the leather cuffs, the only article of clothing between them. His voice is rough when he says, "Lie down on your back," as if he's as affected by all this as Kyle.

He doesn't look to see if Kyle does as he asks, turning his back as he steps into his closet. Kyle obeys, proud that Aidan doesn't need to make sure he's listening, but annoyed because he's already lost Aidan's attention.

He lifts his arms above his head, because he knows it's a good look for him, the long line of his body on display, chest pushed out.

Aidan returns with two more cuffs and a small cardboard box.

"Stay," Aidan says when Kyle starts to sit up. "I'll show you everything."

Kyle settles back against the bed.

Aidan holds up the cuffs. They're brown which means they don't match his wrist cuffs. "These are for your ankles." He tilts the box toward Kyle next. It's full of different hooks and clips and a couple of leather straps with O-rings on either end.

Restraints.

His stomach swoops as if the bottom's dropping, like he's on one of those rides at the amusement park, and he doesn't know when he'll stop falling. Having his wrists and ankles bound—it's not something he can do all the time. It's something that scares him, and he knows Aidan knows that. Kyle's been bound and left before. Is Aidan mad at him? Kyle knows he pushed, but maybe he pushed too far. Maybe—

"Hey," Aidan says, soft. He cups Kyle's cheek to recapture his attention. "I have three options for you. Nod so I know you're with me."

Kyle nods, careful so he doesn't lose Aidan's touch.

"Good." Aidan smiles at him, warm and encouraging. "I have three options for you. "I can use these—" he holds up the straps and clips "—to restrain you. I can use the rope and tie knots that one hard tug will undo. Or we can do something different."

Kyle opens his mouth to answer, automatic, and shuts it again. He looks at the box then looks at Aidan. He doesn't want the third option, he wants to see what Aidan planned. Aidan knows Kyle's limits, which means if he's offered the first two then he won't push Kyle beyond what he's comfortable with.

"If you pick option one or two, then I won't leave the bed until I've unclipped or untied you," Aidan promises.

Kyle's throat is thick with emotions he doesn't want to put a name to. "Option one," he says, and his voice wavers, but it isn't because he's nervous anymore. Aidan will take care of him; all he has to do is let him.

"What are your words?" Aidan asks as he picks up the ankle cuffs.

"Green for good, yellow for slow down, red for stop."

"Use them if you need them."

Aidan waits for Kyle's nod before he buckles the cuffs around Kyle's ankles. He uses the straps to secure Kyle's ankles to the two lower bedposts.

Kyle lifts his arms above his head.

His heart beats fast, almost too fast as Aidan picks up the last two straps. He knows Aidan wants to secure him, but what happens after?

He won't leave me. He promised.

Aidan secures Kyle's wrists. Kyle tugs on his restraints to see how much room he has. Not much. There's no strain in his muscles, he isn't pulled too tight in any direction, but he's stuck. And, with his arms and legs stretching out in different directions, he's *exposed.*

Aidan settles on the bed next to Kyle, lying on his side. He stares, and color floods Kyle's cheeks. He's on display for Aidan, his entire body here for Aidan to look at, to judge. It's good and too much at the same time.

Kyle squirms as much as his bonds allow.

When that doesn't settle the feeling in his stomach, he closes his eyes.

He has a brief moment of relief until Aidan tsks and says, "Open your eyes. This is what you wanted, remember? You wanted to look. So look."

Kyle opens his eyes again and turns his head so he can see Aidan. His hair is still damp in places from his shower, strands sticking wetly together, but it's dry everywhere else. It looks fluffy enough to touch, and Kyle's fingers close around air when he curls them.

He's seen Aidan's face dozens of times now, but his gaze lingers on Aidan's ears then his eyes and the soft bow of his lips. Kyle wants to trace his fingers over Aidan's face, wants to press his lips against Aidan's until he can commit the feel of them to his memory.

His gaze dips down to Aidan's collarbone, and Kyle wants to press his lips there too. He wants to suck kisses there, wants to leave Aidan reminders of them for when Kyle isn't here.

He can't.

When he sees Aidan's nipples for the first time, he tugs on his restraints. He wants to lick them, maybe bite a little to see if Aidan will gasp and tell him to keep going.

He wants to trace his fingers over where Aidan's ribs hide underneath his skin. He wants to press a soft kiss against Aidan's belly button then nuzzle his skin as he follows the wispy trail of hair to his cock.

Kyle looks at Aidan through lowered lashes as his tongue flicks out to wet his lips. He knows what he looks like, has gotten his way more than once by fluttering his lashes just right.

Aidan's unmoved.

"You wanted to look," Aidan says. "I'm letting you look."

"I want to touch too."

"Not right now. You thought you were clever washing all my towels, but you didn't think far enough ahead. You got what you wanted; I'm naked, but you won't touch me, and I won't touch you."

Aidan's right, it's not exactly what Kyle wants, but it's still a pretty good deal. If he looks too happy, will Aidan take this away as well?

"Are those my parameters?" Kyle asks. "No touching?"

"No touching."

Kyle's gaze flicks down to Aidan's cock. "Will you jerk off on me?"

He won't have Aidan's teeth biting marks into his skin, but he can be claimed in this way.

Aidan grabs the lube from his nightstand before he straddles Kyle. He makes sure he's high enough on his knees that his body doesn't touch Kyle's.

"You're really committing to this," Kyle says.

"Discipline's important."

"If I say I'm sorry will you let me suck you?"

"Will you mean it?"

Kyle falls quiet, because one, he won't, and two, Aidan starts stroking himself, and that takes up most of his attention. He doesn't use much lube, enough so he won't chafe, but it isn't an easy slide. Unsurprisingly, Kyle likes the mess of too much lube. He likes it between his fingers and slippery on his cock, likes how he has to wipe it off on his stomach or his thighs if he wants a better grip.

Aidan huffs out a quiet laugh. "Didn't think so. I'm going to get off like this, stroking myself, while you look up at me. After I come on your stomach, we'll eat dinner together. Maybe later, I'll let you come."

"Maybe?"

Aidan's lips curve up into a smile. "Maybe," he repeats. "Now, lie there, and give me something pretty to look at."

Kyle doesn't know whether to scowl or bat his eyelashes. He ends up flushing, cheeks turning pink as Aidan stares at him. He came up with this whole plan to finally see Aidan naked and, somehow, it's him on display. His blush spreads for Aidan to track. His chest rises and falls with short, choppy breaths. He's pinned beneath Aidan, anchored by leather instead of Aidan's touch, but he thinks even without the restraints he wouldn't be able to move.

He was first drawn to Aidan because he wanted his attention. He saw Aidan talking with Lou, saw how he leaned in, saw how he gave his complete focus to the man he was with, and Kyle *wanted*.

He has exactly what he wants. It's almost too much.

"Please," Kyle whispers.

He doesn't know what he's asking for. He doesn't have any more plans, didn't think this one through far enough. He's here beneath Aidan, Aidan's cock hard and leaking, and Kyle needs *something*. He trusts Aidan to know what it is.

He pulls against his restraints to feel how he's been caught. The cuffs around his wrists remind him that Aidan put him here. The snug circle of leather almost feels as though it's Aidan holding him down.

Kyle's eyelids flutter, but they don't shut. Aidan wants him to watch.

Wants to watch in return.

"Please," he asks again.

Aidan's rhythm stutters. He squeezes his cock too tight and groans. "I wanted to keep you here longer."

"You can have me whenever you want." Kyle will drape himself across Aidan's bed whenever the man asks. He won't even need to be restrained. Maybe next time, they'll touch each other.

Aidan shakes his head, as if he can't quite believe it.

They don't speak again as Aidan resumes stroking himself, quicker now. He twists his wrist on each upstroke, and he tips his head back as he gets close, but he never breaks eye contact. It makes Kyle feel like a part of this even though there isn't a single place they're touching.

When Aidan comes, a warm splatter across Kyle's skin, Kyle smiles.

Aidan falls forward, his hands still on either side of Kyle but closer than he was before. A little more and Aidan could tuck his face against Kyle's neck. He could slide his hands into Kyle's hair or press kisses to his cheeks. He could—

Move away?

Aidan shuffles down the bed, *away*, but before Kyle can vocalize how much he doesn't want this, Aidan's fingers are on his ankle straps. He undoes the one on the left then the one on the right.

"Pull your knees up," Aidan says.

Kyle obeys, tucking his knees close to his chest before he stretches his legs out again.

"Everything feel good?" Aidan asks.

At Kyle's nod, Aidan moves to Kyle's wrists. He undoes these straps as well, leaving Kyle in his cuffs, but with a new freedom of movement.

"Arms now."

Kyle draws his arms in then stretches them out. He nods. Everything's in working order.

He reaches a hand out, but he stops before he touches Aidan's face. "May I?"

It's Aidan's turn to nod.

Kyle cups Aidan's cheek then slides his hand around to the back of Aidan's neck. He pulls him closer and Aidan lets him. He closes the distance between them until they're pressed together, head to foot.

Does it mean his punishment is over? Is he forgiven? Kyle spreads his legs so Aidan falls between them. He hooks his ankles together behind Aidan's back, his turn to hold Aidan in place.

"We can't stay like this for long," Aidan says. "We need a shower."

Kyle shakes his head. He doesn't want to move. He wants Aidan pressed up against him, warm, solid, *here*.

"Ten minutes," Aidan says. "Then we have to shower. We should eat too."

"Dinner then shower."

Kyle doesn't want to give up his cuffs yet. Though there's one set he wouldn't mind losing.

He unhooks his ankles.

"We don't have to go now," Aidan says. "We can stay a little longer."

"I want these off," Kyle says.

Aidan sits up, a small frown wrinkling his forehead, but he unbuckles Kyle's ankle cuffs for him. When he reaches for Kyle's wrists, Kyle shakes his head.

"These are mine. I want them to stay."

The frown eases. "Okay," Aidan says. "Let me get something to wipe us up with and I'll be back."

"I'm not going anywhere," Kyle promises.

Chapter Eleven

AFTER DINNER, KYLE does the dishes while Aidan takes care of the laundry. There's a neat stack of folded clothes and a mess of towels when Kyle joins Aidan in the living room.

"Hold these," Aidan says before he scoops up the towels and drops them in Kyle's arms.

"I'm not sure we need all these for our shower," Kyle says. There are hand towels and facecloths and dish towels mixed in with the bath towels. One of the facecloths slips off the top of the pile. It lands on Kyle's foot, and he kicks it up in the air then catches it between his pinky and ring fingers.

He glances at Aidan to see if he noticed.

"Am I supposed to be impressed?" Aidan asks, but a smile tugs at his lips.

"I have all kinds of hidden skills. What am I doing with these?"

Aidan leads him into the bathroom, where Kyle dumps his armload on the counter while Aidan turns on the shower. They fold towels side by side, shoulders brushing, and it's domestic in a way that makes Kyle's chest ache.

Aidan leaves two towels out for their shower and pulls his shirt over his head.

Kyle follows suit, losing his shirt, then his pants. He hesitates when he's naked, because his cuffs are still on and he can't get in the shower with them. But he doesn't want to take them off.

Aidan pulls back the shower curtain, and he has one foot in the shower when he realizes Kyle isn't moving.

His gaze flicks to Kyle's wrists. "Ah," he says.

"Yeah." Kyle's voice sounds as heavy as it feels.

Aidan steps out of the shower. "May I?" he asks.

Kyle holds his wrists out for Aidan. Aidan takes his time unbuckling them, fingers sweeping across Kyle's skin, touching him more than he needs to. Kyle sways closer to him. When Aidan's done, Kyle's wrists are bare only for a moment before Aidan circles his fingers around the left one.

"Is this okay?" Aidan asks.

Kyle stares at where Aidan's holding him. He nods, head quieting again now that Aidan's firmly in control. Maybe it's selfish for Kyle to want this. Maybe he shouldn't need it. But Aidan's offering, so Kyle nods.

They step into the shower together, and there's enough space for them to stand comfortably apart. Kyle presses himself against Aidan once they're both in, because he doesn't want that space. He understands why Aidan wants them to shower, but Kyle doesn't want distance between them.

Compromise.

It's what relationships are about, right?

"Can I wash you?" Aidan asks, something vulnerable in his words.

Maybe Kyle isn't the only one still feeling the effects of earlier. Kyle steps even closer then turns so he's standing under the spray of water. Using his free hand, Aidan tilts Kyle's head back so the water runs through his hair.

"Here." Aidan places the shampoo bottle in Kyle's hands then holds his own hand out, palm up.

Kyle squeezes a bit into Aidan's hand. It's strange having his hair washed with only one hand. He's not sure his hair gets particularly clean, but it doesn't matter. He showered this morning. He closes his eyes as Aidan's fingers rub small circles against his scalp. He draws even breaths as Aidan rinses his hair. He leans into Aidan when he reaches around him to turn the water off.

Aidan dries him off, starting with his ankles and working his way up. Kyle's as naked as he was earlier on his bed, but he doesn't want to hide from Aidan's attention this time. His hands are loose in Aidan's hair, because Aidan needs both his hands to dry Kyle, and he isn't ready to give up their connection yet.

He doesn't think he'll be going home tonight.

He wants to spend the night in Aidan's bed, tucked close to him. As Aidan dries his thighs then moves up toward Kyle's stomach, he thinks they don't even need to have sex again. Somewhere between Aidan coming on him and now, Kyle's lost his erection. With some effort, he could bring it back, but he doesn't necessarily want to.

Aidan pauses, towel sagging as he looks up at Kyle from his knees.

Objectively, it's a breathtaking sight.

Maybe if Kyle still had some of today's earlier brattiness, then he'd smirk or flirt, but now, he simply meets Aidan's gaze evenly.

"I'm not—I don't—" Kyle falls silent. He's not sure how to say what he's thinking without it being insulting. Sometimes, being taken care of makes him hard. Other times, like this, it has a different effect. There's a bubble of calm around him, one he doesn't want to burst.

"You had plans," he finally says. He doesn't want to make this decision. He's not sure he can ask Aidan to make it either. His fingers tremble in Aidan's hair.

"I can adjust them," Aidan says.

The steam from the shower is dissipating, leaving the droplets of water on Kyle's skin to chill. "Can we—bed?"

Aidan nods. He finishes drying Kyle off and drops the towel on the floor to be dealt with later. He picks up one of Kyle's cuffs. "May I?"

Kyle thrusts his wrist out, almost punching Aidan's stomach in the process. They both laugh, a quiet chuckle.

"Guess that's a yes," Aidan says.

He buckles one cuff then the other, and Kyle has to close his eyes, overwhelmed once they're both on. He has the steady comfort of leather wrapped around his wrists. Soon, he'll have Aidan touching him again. It'll be too much in the best of ways.

When he opens his eyes again, Aidan's still in front of him, watching, steady.

"I want you," Kyle says. Feelings and words bubble up inside him, faster than he can process. "I want you on me, *in* me. I need you so badly. Please, I—" He falters as Aidan pulls him into the bedroom, but he finds his voice again as soon as they're on his bed. "Will you fuck me? I need you inside me. I need you as close as you can be. *Please.*"

"All you have to do is ask."

Aidan fumbles with his bedside drawer before he jerks it open. He tosses the bottle of lube onto the bed then groans and heads into his closet.

Kyle needs Aidan in him *now*. He slicks up his fingers, because the sooner he's prepped, the sooner Aidan can fuck him. Aidan makes a small sound and Kyle looks up to see him standing in the doorway of the closet, his toy box in hand, and his mouth hanging open.

He snaps his mouth shut with an audible click. Heat and longing fill his gaze. Kyle spreads his legs more to show off his body, to show how much space there is for Aidan here.

"You were taking too long," Kyle says, whines really, if he's being honest with himself. He's loose but not too loose. Aidan could fuck him now if he wanted. It all depends on how tight he wants Kyle to be. If he was slow then he doesn't need to stretch Kyle anymore.

Aidan crosses the room in three long strides, and he drops his box on the nightstand with a clatter.

Kyle starts to pull his fingers out, but Aidan puts his fingers on his wrist. "I want you to help me. Show me what you were doing while I couldn't see you."

He slides his fingers back in, Aidan's grip still tight on his cuff. This isn't the best angle to get his fingers deep, but he can spread them, making room inside himself for Aidan.

"Hold them like that," Aidan says when Kyle's fingers are scissored open.

Then Aidan presses one of his fingers between Kyle's. In one sharp exhale, he loses all the oxygen in his lungs and all the thoughts in his head. He's transfixed by the sight of Aidan's finger as it disappears into his body. He can feel the slide of Aidan's finger against his, then the push as it reaches deeper than Kyle's can.

His eyes sting because it's been so long since he blinked. He blinks three times in rapid succession to keep from tearing up. When he refocuses, he's not looking at where their fingers touch. He's looking at where their wrists touch, at his cuff and how Aidan's hand brushes against it every time he moves.

"Now," Kyle says, voice hoarse. "Fuck me *now*. Please."

"Okay," Aidan says, but he pulls his finger out slowly, as if he doesn't want to stop touching Kyle.

It's stupid, because if he hurried then his dick could be in Kyle and that definitely counts as touching. Kyle shifts on the bed, restless, needing more than he has. He itches to grasp two fistfuls of Aidan's hair and drag him where he wants the man, but he closes his hands around two fistfuls of the sheets instead.

He regrets it as soon as Aidan moves away, which is the wrong direction. What is he doing?

Kyle whines, past words now.

"I've got you," Aidan promises as he pulls out a condom. "Just a minute."

Kyle doesn't want to wait a minute. He's empty and Aidan isn't even touching him anymore. Aidan promised him anything he asked for. Well, he's asked, and Aidan hasn't given him what he wants.

"Please," Kyle says. "Please."

"I've got you," Aidan says again. "Turn on your side for me, okay?"

He turns on his side, even though part of him doesn't want to. He wants to see Aidan while he fucks him. He wants Aidan to bury himself deep, then drag him down for a kiss.

Aidan lies down behind him and arranges them until he can slide into Kyle. This—this is better than Kyle hoped for. They're touching from their shoulders to their feet, Aidan's toes resting against the bottom of Kyle's feet.

Aidan presses kisses to Kyle's neck and shoulders, any bit of skin he can reach without having to move. He rolls his hips, slow, not in any kind of rush. He doesn't pull out far, as if he doesn't want to put even that much distance between himself and Kyle.

He wraps his arm around Kyle's waist, not to pull him back but so his fingers can stroke over the cuff on Kyle's wrist.

Kyle trembles in Aidan's hold, because *this* is everything he wanted, and Aidan's given it to him like he promised. There's a towel and a bottle of juice on the bedside table, because after they're done, Aidan doesn't want to go far. Aidan's filled him up, wrapped himself around him, and Kyle feels held, protected, *wanted.*

Tears rise in Kyle's eyes and he's glad they're not face to face.

Aidan rocks into him, slow, gentle, something that might put Kyle to sleep if he weren't so determined not to miss a single second of this. He knows what a look from under his eyelashes will get him, knows what to expect when he sinks to his knees. He knows how to flirt, and flaunt himself, and the best way to ensure his Dom will press bruises into his skin.

He doesn't know how to get this.

Sweet. Tender.

They've been pressed together so long that Kyle's back is sweating. Aidan's chest slides against his skin, and by now, he's kissed every available bit of Kyle's skin, but he just starts over from the beginning.

He slips his fingers under Kyle's cuff, as if he needs to be touching skin and leather at the same time. Or maybe he's remembering the shower when it had been his fingers tethering Kyle to him.

All of it together is too much, or maybe not enough, because when Aidan comes and pulls out, Kyle whimpers at being empty again. He's empty and his back is cold because Aidan's moving away. There's no longer a hand on his wrist, and his cuff feels too loose.

Kyle turns on his stomach to bury his face in his pillow. *Selfish. Greedy. Demanding.*

"Hey," Aidan says, his voice barely above a whisper. He rests a hand on Kyle's shoulder. "I was tossing the condom, but I'm back now. I'm not going anywhere."

Away. Tossed condom means they're done. Kyle tightens up, and he slides his hands under the pillow where Aidan can't reach them. He doesn't want to give up his cuffs. He doesn't want to give up any of this.

Aidan pats Kyle's back with the towel. "Is this good or do you want me to wet a washcloth?"

Kyle shakes his head. He doesn't want Aidan to leave. He wants Aidan touching him again. He wants the weight of his body pinning him to the bed. He wants to feel safe again. Cherished.

"All right," Aidan says. His fingers stroke down Kyle's back, raising goose bumps on his arms. "I won't go anywhere. Is there anything else you want?"

Kyle turns his face from his pillow, because words. Words are how he gets what he wants. "I want you in me."

"Fingers or plug?"

There's no judgement on how needy Kyle's being, no rejection either.

"Fingers."

When Aidan slides two fingers into him, Kyle breathes out, the last piece of what he needs slotting into place. He sinks into the mattress, every bit of tension slipping out of him.

"This was good," Kyle says, his voice heavy and thick with sleep. "We'll talk later."

"Okay," Aidan says. He presses a kiss to Kyle's shoulder then the back of his neck.

It's how Kyle falls asleep, with Aidan's fingers filling him and Aidan's lips on his skin.

It's his new favorite way to fall asleep.

Chapter Twelve

KYLE RETURNS TO his apartment Sunday night, because Aidan has class in the morning, and he, flatteringly, told Kyle that he "wouldn't be able to force himself out of bed if Kyle was in it."

So Kyle drives home after dinner and bakes a full batch of cookies, because it's that or examine his feelings.

Cookies are easier.

By the time they're cool enough to put on a plate, Kyle's chest squeezes his heart as if his body can eject it if it only applies enough force.

Kyle takes the cookies over to Jenny and Charlotte.

He throws the door open and announces, "I'm having feelings."

Both women look up from their dinner.

Jenny rolls her eyes. "You've had feelings since the beginning."

"Yeah, but these are *feelings*."

Jenny holds her hands out expectantly for the cookies. Kyle hands them over then sits next to Charlotte, because she's the nice one out of the two.

"You were gone all weekend," Charlotte says. "That's a good sign. He probably has feelings too."

"He does." Aidan's genuinely happy every time he sees him, but that could easily be because every time he sees Kyle they're either about to have amazing sex or plan amazing sex. Or talk about the amazing sex they just had. "That doesn't mean they're *feelings*."

Jenny groans. "Is this seriously the conversation we're having right now? I was more articulate when I was in middle school." She plucks two cookies from the plate and stacks them on top of each other before she takes a bite.

"You wrote anonymous notes and left them in Mary's locker," Kyle reminds her. "She thought they were from David, and that's how Mary and David became the power couple of Kennedy Middle School."

"The takeaway from this story is that I was so good at writing notes that if I signed my name then I could've dated Mary."

"Except Mary hated you. That's why you didn't sign your name in the first place, because if she saw it, then she would've torn up the notes."

"She liked me just fine." Jenny takes another bite of her cookies and chocolate smears across her mouth.

"You literally pulled her pigtails. You did it so often that over winter break she got a pixie cut."

"She looked cute with a pixie cut."

"She did, but that's not the point." What even was Kyle's point?

"If you don't want to talk about Aidan's feelings, then do you want to talk about yours?" Charlotte asks.

Jenny groans again, as if she'd hoped to distract Kyle and now Charlotte's ruined her plans.

"We showered together," Kyle says. Jenny makes another noise, this one more like *why are you telling me this*? He rolls his eyes. He isn't about to give her details. She knows him better than that. "I didn't want to take my cuffs off."

Jenny drops her cookies on the table. "Shit. *Those* kind of feelings?"

"I suck at casual."

"I'm glad you've found someone who's made you so happy," Charlotte says because she really is the nice one. She pulls the cookies toward him. "Have a few, you'll feel better."

"Yeah." Kyle takes a cookie and bites into it so he doesn't tell them more.

So he doesn't tell them how he spent Friday night as close to Aidan as he possibly could or how he spent Saturday afternoon kneeling next to the couch while Aidan graded papers because he still didn't want any distance between them. He doesn't tell them about how he cried on Friday night, not *I've been spanked so hard I'm crying* tears, but *I'm falling in love with my scene partner and I don't know what to do* tears.

AFTER THE CLOSENESS of the weekend, the next week is tough. On Monday, they text back and forth, but Aidan has a couple of students make appointments, so they don't see each other Monday night.

On Tuesday, Aidan goes out with his department and his texts to Kyle are scattered.

Wednesday, Aidan attends a guest lecture at his school, and Kyle doesn't care much for poetry, but he would've listened to a poetry reading if it meant seeing Aidan. But maybe Aidan didn't want to see *him*. Or be seen with him.

By Thursday, Kyle's feeling down, and it doesn't help when Aidan says no to hanging out because he has to go to the grocery store. He's had a busy week so maybe 8:00 p.m. is the only time he can go to the store, but Kyle would rather Aidan see *him*.

It's a disappointing week, but Kyle knows not everyone's schedule is as flexible as his. And at least they'll have the weekend together.

"I'll be out of town tonight," Aidan says when Kyle calls him at his lunch break on Friday. "I'm sorry."

"You're a busy guy," Kyle says. He hopes he keeps the bitterness out of his voice.

"I'm all yours Saturday," Aidan promises. "I'll make it up to you."

He sounds determined and nervous, a strange mix.

"There's nothing to make up," Kyle says. That sounds too much like owning and owning means he's doing something because he thinks he has to and not because he wants to. "Text me when you wake up, and we can figure out our plans."

"I'll be up early."

"Even after a late night?"

"Yes." Aidan sounds determined again. "Does 10:00 a.m. work?"

In Kyle's book, ten isn't particularly early, but he says, "Yeah, I'll see you then. Your place or mine?"

"Mine."

Kyle nods. Whatever Aidan has planned—and he's planning something—he wants to be in his own house for it. "Do you mind if I go to the club tonight? Not to pick up or anything, obviously." He bites his lip and wonders why he's suddenly so wrong-footed. "Just to hang."

"Of course, you can go. Say hi to TJ for me."

"On a Friday night?" Kyle laughs.

They talk for a little bit longer, but Aidan has class, and Kyle needs to work some more. He's been fairly productive this week, but he's determined to spend all of Saturday with Aidan. Sunday too if he can swing it.

HE'S JUST FINISHED his final drafts for the library fundraiser when Jenny flings his door open.

"You're not being sad and boring tonight," she declares. "You're coming out."

"Sorry, already out." Kyle flashes a grin.

Jenny lifts her eyes to the ceiling. "Get dressed or we're leaving without you."

"Tell me I'm funny first."

Jenny flips him off instead, and he laughs all the way back to his room.

It takes him some time to pick out an outfit that looks good but doesn't imply he's trying to hook up tonight.

When he's done, Charlotte's joined Jenny in his living room.

"Hey," she says.

"I finished the stuff for the library and emailed it to Mrs. Manion."

"You can call her Edith."

"She's three times my age, which means we're not on a first name basis." Charlotte smiles at him. "Okay."

"Don't leave without me tonight," Kyle tells the women as he locks up his apartment. "You're my ride home."

"Oh?" Jenny asks. "Flying solo tonight?"

"I'm not solo." He's very much taken. Unless...no. Aidan's had a busy week, that's all. There's no need for Kyle to jump to worst-case scenarios. He and Aidan are good. They *are*.

"Riiight," Jenny says.

"Is Aidan busy again?" Charlotte asks, the slightest hint of disapproval in her voice.

"Yeah, but I'm seeing him tomorrow." He gives each woman a pointed look.

"We should do dinner, the four of us," Charlotte says as she leads them down to the parking lot. "Or maybe we can sign up for one of those bar trivia nights. They always want teams of four and we'd kick ass."

"You and Aidan would," Kyle says. "But I wouldn't mind cheering you on."

"Mozzarella sticks?" Jenny asks, hopeful.

Charlotte pats her girlfriend's arm. "You can have a whole order to yourself this time."

"I'm in. When are we going?"

THE CLUB IS packed when they arrive. It's the kind of Friday night throng Kyle loves. There will never be a lack of people to talk to, and he'll have to fight for a spot at the bar. It's all cramming into booths and squeezing between people to cross the room. It's being near other people without any kind of flirtation or expectation behind it.

There are familiar faces everywhere he turns and a few new ones as well as Kyle picks a place near the bar to stand. There's a wall of people at least four deep between him and any hope of being noticed so he shuffles closer to the woman next to him.

"I haven't seen you before," he says with a grin. "Don't come here often?"

The woman groans before she even turns to face him. "I don't know if it's worse if you meant that or if you're joking. Either you aren't smooth or you have a terrible sense of humor."

Kyle grins and notes the studs lining her eyebrows.

He briefly had an ear pierced at the insistence of a boyfriend. He always gave Kyle a new earring for things like their three-month anniversary and his birthday. Kyle's pretty sure it was because Mike was too unimaginative to come up with anything else.

After they broke up, Kyle didn't bother with the piercing anymore.

Jenny has a bunch, but which ones she wears depends on how she feels when she wakes up in the morning and what kind of client meetings are on her schedule.

"I'm both smooth and have a fantastic sense of humor," Kyle says. "I'm Kyle, by the way."

"Caitlin. And to answer your earlier question; no, I haven't been here often. Tonight's my first time, and if you want to make a joke about that, then I'll point out I'm in five-inch heels."

Kyle looks down and—yep, those are five-inch heels with a wicked point on them. "Impressive."

"I'd ask you if you want to try them, but you don't seem like that's your thing."

"No. Nothing sexy about me breaking an ankle."

"They're not bad once you practice."

"There are other things I'd rather spend my time practicing." He glances at her shoes again, because, seriously, *impressive*. "But if you're searching for someone to practice with, then I can introduce you to a few people. Or if you only want to look tonight, then that's cool too."

"Is that what you're doing?" Caitlin tucks her hair behind her ear. "Looking?"

A few people, drinks in hand, squeeze their way out of the bar crowd. Kyle quickly steps into the space they left behind and pulls Caitlin along with him.

"I'm mostly here for the conversation," Kyle says, and he turns another bright smile on her, brighter now that he doesn't have to worry about leading her on.

"My friend recommended this place," Caitlin says. "It's much better than the last place he sent me. It was a bar filled with too much smoke and not enough people on the same page as me."

"You'll definitely find people here with similar interests," Kyle promises. "Are you interested in guys? Girls? Both?"

"Both but mostly guys."

Kyle narrows down the list of people he has in his head. "Is it the crossdressing you like? The control? The practicing?"

Kyle could get onboard with the last one. He wonders if Caitlin would laugh at him if he got it wrong. Would she steady him when he wobbled or tell him to be better? He bets he can find a way to work this into a scene with Aidan. Not the heels. Kyle isn't interested in that side of the equation. But Kyle fumbling to do something right and Aidan gently mocking him? He's definitely interested in *that*.

Caitlin laughs, open and friendly. "You sound like the survey I filled out earlier."

"But better because it'll take Wanda some time to match you with people worth talking to, and I can give you some suggestions before we even have our drinks."

Caitlin raises her eyebrows. "You're on a first name basis with the owner?"

"We're friends, but don't let that intimidate you. I'm still the guy you happened to meet at the bar."

"With a terrible sense of humor," Caitlin says, smiling again.

They've finally made it to the bar, but they haven't seen TJ or Derek, the two bartenders on tonight. That's when someone drapes an arm around Kyle's waist.

"Hey, babe," Alexa says, leaning on him. She glances at Caitlin. "I hope he isn't bothering you."

"He's not. Uh, I'm Caitlin." She starts to hold out her hand then pulls it back. "We've been having a nice talk, actually."

"Wow," Alexa says, enough surprise in her voice that Kyle elbows her. She only laughs. "Richard's doing a scene later, if you want to watch."

"Spanking again?" He's curious to see how far Richard's come since his and Kyle's scene a couple months ago.

"Flogging," Alexa says.

"Shame. He has nice hands."

Alexa laughs and pats Kyle's hip. "I'll take your word on that one. Have you seen Rex around?"

"No, you have something planned?"

"I'm hoping to, if his schedule's free."

Rex is well over six feet tall and built like the bouncer he is. He's by far Alexa's favorite scene partner. She's five and a half feet tall on a good day, and there's nothing she loves more than putting bigger guys on their knees and making them beg for her strap-on.

Kyle's a little jealous of Rex right now. Alexa might be small, but she makes up for it by being absolutely ruthless. Kyle's scalp tingled for days after the last time he scened with her. He wouldn't mind a rough scene tonight. He's aching for marks that'll last, for something to look at or bruises to press on when he doesn't have Aidan.

Alexa flicks his ear. "Stop looking so starry-eyed. I'd make you an offer if you weren't already taken."

"I'd say yes."

"That's because you're easy." She goes up on her tiptoes to kiss his cheek. "If you see Rex, will you tell him I'm looking for him?"

"Of course. Have a good night."

She grins before melting back into the crowd.

"That's Alexa," Kyle tells Caitlin, because Alexa didn't introduce herself. "She's into making guys cry on her fake dick. So, if that's something you're interested in, then I'm sure she'd let you sit in on a scene."

Color rises in Caitlin's cheeks.

"Oh," Kyle says. "When you said first time, I thought you meant first time here. You meant *first time*."

Caitlin shrugs, suddenly shy. "My friend thought I was less likely to get signals wrong if I met guys here rather than in a regular bar or something. Not that this isn't regular. Um—"

"It's fine," he promises. "But yeah, Alexa's great. I'll give you a better introduction when she isn't on a mission."

Their conversation is interrupted by TJ setting two beers on the counter, one for Kyle and one for Aidan. He's gone before Kyle can say anything.

"I guess you really aren't new here," Caitlin says. "You have a standing order."

Kyle swallows past the lump in his throat. "Either of them look good to you?"

She takes Kyle's favorite which leaves him with Aidan's. Kyle ignores his brain as it tries to bring his mood down. "Want to find someplace to sit?"

"Sure." They find a booth that's too big for just the two of them, but it's the only open seating they could find. "So, two beers and Alexa said you were taken. I can do the math. Where's your man? Woman?"

"He's away tonight. Work, I think."

Caitlin nods. She looks around the room, eyes growing wider as she tries to take everything in. After a minute, she drops her gaze back to the table. "So, uh, what do you like?"

"You do not want to open that can of worms," Lou says, appearing at their table.

He's brought Cynthia and Jamaal with him, and Kyle slides over to make room.

"Caitlin, this is Lou. He's sometimes my friend but not tonight, because he's being mean." Kyle drags Lou in for a loud kiss on his cheek. "This is Cynthia. She's the nicest person you'll meet at Enchanting Encounters. And that's Jamaal. He doesn't like me."

"You talk too much," Jamaal says.

"Matter of opinion," Kyle says. "Are you guys staying a while?"

The three settle into the booth, and Kyle's finally able to relax.

HE'S A LITTLE drunk when he gets home. He won't have a hangover tomorrow, but his filter's pretty much gone which is what he blames on the text he sends Aidan.

He's brushed his teeth and is in his bed with all the lights out when he pulls up his text conversation with Aidan.

KYLE: *I missed you tonight. The club isn't as fun without you.*

It's *true,* but even as he hits send he knows he'll regret saying it in the morning.

Aidan texts back almost immediately.

AIDAN: *I missed you too. See you tomorrow.*

Kyle reads the text three times to make sure it isn't just wishful thinking then he curls up around his phone. It's another thing he'll regret in the morning, but it isn't morning yet.

He falls asleep with Aidan's words running through his head.

Chapter Thirteen

KYLE WAKES UP too early to head over to Aidan's, so he works out then takes a long shower. He makes himself a full breakfast and still has an hour to watch TV. He doesn't want to look desperate by going over too early, but it's a struggle to wait until quarter of ten.

Because he *is* desperate. A week is a long time to go without seeing Aidan. He tries not to think about how if a week without each other makes him this miserable, then it'll be even worse when they stop scening together.

They're a month into their three-month partnership. Maybe they'll extend it again, but maybe they won't. Kyle's stomach twists unpleasantly, and he regrets eating so much at breakfast.

His nausea lingers even when he arrives at Aidan's. What if this is the end already? Maybe this week's distance has been purposeful. Maybe he invited Kyle over today to gently break up with him.

Kyle thought things were good, but maybe he's been too focused on himself.

He sits in Aidan's driveway for a few minutes, keys still in the ignition, engine running, while he tries to talk himself into going inside. If this is a breakup, then Kyle doesn't want to do it in person.

He'd rather do it over the phone so it's easier for him to curl up on his bed afterwards. Or maybe they could do it via text, because then Aidan wouldn't be able to hear the hitch in Kyle's voice when he says things are over.

Either way, Kyle doesn't like in-person breakups. Maybe he should call Aidan from the driveway and find out what his plans for the day are.

That seems too pathetic.

Kyle turns his car off then heads up the steps to the front door on Aidan's side of the house.

Aidan isn't waiting by the front door when Kyle enters. It's another check in the "breaking up" box.

Voices drift from the kitchen. Kyle's tempted to stomp his feet, tempted to storm out, because he's waited an entire week to see Aidan and he's invited someone else over? Aidan promised a day with just the two of them.

Kyle's smile is strained as he waves to Ritchie.

From what Kyle's seen of Ritchie, Aidan's colleague and neighbor, he isn't known for his tact or his observational skills which only makes it half of a surprise when he takes a look at Kyle and says, "You look like shit."

Kyle shrugs. "Late night."

"I can make you a smoothie for that."

"I'm good but thank you."

Ritchie nods, taking his words at face value. Aidan's gaze lingers, concerned, but Kyle tries to shrug the look off.

"Well, I have to go," Ritchie says. "I'm taking my more dedicated students to a community farm today. We're helping with the harvest."

"Sounds like fun." He waves to Ritchie as the man troops out then laughs when he returns for his coffee mug.

It's quiet after Ritchie leaves. Kyle waits to see if he'll come back again then, as if it's been too long, he stays quiet.

"He dropped by for breakfast," Aidan says, part-explanation and part-apology. Kyle doesn't need either. This is Aidan's house. He's allowed to do whatever he wants in it.

"He was probably afraid you'd starve without him."

"I would've starved with him. He made spinach and feta omelets. Why would you ruin eggs that way?"

"Okay," Kyle says. Then, "I didn't have a late night," because apparently, they both need to justify themselves this morning. He winces as soon as the words are out. What happened to the ease between them?

"It's fine if you did. And fine if you didn't."

"I know," Kyle says, snappier than he means. He takes a deep breath and scrubs at his eyes. "Sorry. I—sorry."

"It's okay," Aidan says, slowly, as if he's weighing his words now. "Do you want some coffee?"

"I'm good, thank you."

Aidan nods, then pours himself another cup of coffee. Kyle wishes he'd said yes so he'd have something to do with his hands.

"I'm going to have a bowl of cereal, because that omelet was seriously disgusting. Are you hungry?"

"I ate already."

If it was another morning, Kyle would offer to make Aidan something, but he can't stand the idea of pushing eggs around a skillet while he wonders if this is the last time he'll be able to do it.

More accurately, he can't stand the idea of watching Aidan eat breakfast while he wonders if they'll still be together in half an hour.

"Are you unhappy?" Kyle asks.

It's a good thing Aidan took his cereal out first and not his bowl, because when he drops it the box bounces harmlessly on the ground.

"What?"

He looks surprised enough, *hurt* enough, that Kyle thinks maybe they won't break up tonight.

"Nothing," Kyle says. "Just—everything's fine."

"Clearly not." Aidan leaves his cereal on the floor. "You think I'm unhappy?"

He takes a step toward Kyle then thinks better of it and stays on his side of the island. Kyle's on the other side, only a couple feet away, but it feels like much more.

"You went shopping at eight o'clock," Kyle says. "You don't even eat real food."

Aidan opens his mouth then closes it. "I did actually go to the store, but yes, I used it as an excuse."

Kyle nods, stomach sinking. He knew this was coming. He hates that he prepared himself for it and it's still managed to catch him off guard.

"Not the way you're thinking," Aidan says. "I wanted to surprise you with something, and I was afraid that if I saw you then I wouldn't be able to keep it a secret."

"You avoided me for a whole week."

Aidan winces. "That—it doesn't sound good when you say it like that."

Kyle doesn't think there's any way to make that sound good, but Aidan at least had the right intentions, even if his execution was terrible. "Is that where you were last night? Getting the surprise?"

"Yes, but I think it's best if I hold on to it for a bit."

"Okay." Kyle's curious but he's still off-balance enough he doesn't want to push. He glances at the cereal box lying on the floor. "Do you want me to make you something?"

"Cereal's fine."

Aidan scoops the box off the floor and pours himself a bowl. He sits at the counter and Kyle sits next to him. There's still too much distance between them but Kyle's not sure how to close it.

"How was your night?" Aidan asks.

"Pretty good. I met a Domme new to the official scene. She's done some spontaneous stuff, but her friend recommended Enchanting Encounters, and I think once she's comfortable she'll love it."

"Oh." Aidan flips a couple of Mini-Wheats over so the milk can soak through both sides. "Was she...nice?"

"In a friendly kind of way. Our interests don't line up, if that's what you're really asking."

Aidan doesn't say anything, which Kyle takes as confirmation.

"But talking with her gave me an idea of something I want to try with you. We should hold off on it for a bit, though." Anything involving even light humiliation is a bad idea when Kyle's feeling this raw.

"Okay. I—" Aidan takes a bite of cereal. "My original plans for today are also on hold. What should we do?"

Earlier this week, Kyle would've said he wants to spend the whole day in bed or on the couch. He isn't in the mood for sex right now, and he isn't up for anything as intimate as cuddling or as domestic as being in Aidan's house together.

"Movie? And then a walk?"

A movie will give them something to talk about on their walk, and they clearly need help there. They're both feeling off, and Kyle wants their normal back.

"Movie and a walk sounds good. Do you want to look up showtimes? If there's anything showing soon, I'll just have one bowl of cereal, then popcorn at the movie."

Kyle laughs as he pulls out his phone.

"I know you're judging me, but we're taking a walk afterwards. That means I can eat whatever I want."

"Sure," Kyle says. He flashes Aidan a smile before looking at his phone again.

He picks an action movie which promises rooftop chase scenes and explosions, because he's not in the mood for anything heavy or emotional.

"You're in luck," Kyle says. "There's an 11:15 showing. You can enjoy a lunch of buttered popcorn and slushies."

"Are slushies your weakness, then?" Aidan finishes his cereal then drinks the milk from his bowl.

Kyle can't help but move away from him. "People willingly do that?"

Aidan raises his eyebrows, bowl still in hand.

"My babysitter used to force me to drink the milk out of my bowl," Kyle explains.

"Sounds like a traumatic experience."

"I don't eat cereal anymore."

It's Aidan's turn to look baffled. "What do you do when you're running late in the morning?"

"I'm self-employed, so I'm never running late. But if I'm in a rush, then I'll do yogurt and granola or throw a bunch of fruit into my blender and make a smoothie."

Aidan rinses his bowl and his spoon and sets them on the drying rack. "I guess that makes sense."

"Speaking of throwing food together, why don't I toss some stuff in your Crockpot so we have something to eat after our walk. Unless—" *That's too much time to spend together.* Kyle bites down on the words before he says them aloud, but from the hurt that flashes across Aidan's face, the point still came across.

"That sounds good," Aidan says. "I'm not sure I have anything that'll work, but you're more than welcome to anything you find."

"I used to play this game with my college roommates." Kyle opens his fridge and his freezer so he can take inventory. "At the end of the semester, we'd empty out our kitchen and cook everything."

"We did the same thing, but with alcohol."

Kyle takes out a bag of frozen carrots, a bag of frozen corn, and a tray of chicken. He grabs the salsa from the fridge and a couple of other things. "The best was at the end of the spring semester, because we'd take everything we had and meet-up with a bunch of other people at the local park. We'd grill and have a giant potluck picnic."

Kyle pokes around the pantry until he has a neat collection of ingredients on the counter. "Have you ever had taco soup?"

Aidan shakes his head. "I thought they were a solid food."

"Not today. Usually, I'd use ground beef, but I know you don't like it. Honestly, I'm surprised you have chicken breasts."

Aidan shrugs and he ducks his head, embarrassed. The only reason for him to be embarrassed would be if—

"Did you stock your house for when I came over?"

"You enjoy cooking," Aidan says, "and I never have anything."

So he went to the store this week to buy a bunch of random shit because he thought it would make Kyle happy.

"You're an idiot," Kyle tells him. "A cute idiot that I really like, but you're an idiot."

Aidan nods, accepting the label.

Kyle abandons the food to brush a kiss over Aidan's cheek. "Do you want to help me?"

"Will I mess it up?"

"It's pretty hard to mess up dumping shit in a Crockpot."

"Then sure," Aidan says.

KYLE BUYS THEIR tickets at the theater while Aidan investigates the concession stand, which turns out to be a mistake. When Kyle joins him at the counter, Aidan has the largest tub of popcorn Kyle has ever seen.

"You'll make yourself sick eating all of that," Kyle says.

"Which is why we're sharing." Aidan grins. "Red or blue slushie?"

"Red, please. And a small one or I'll spend the whole movie shivering."

The girl behind the counter smiles at them as she puts a cup under the slushie spout. "It's a good excuse to cuddle, though. I always get the ice cream bites when I go to the movies with my boyfriend. Of course, it took him three movies before he stopped bringing me an extra coat. It's a good thing I can see movies for free, because he's clueless."

"I think we're a little old for cuddling in the back of movie theaters," Kyle says.

"You're never too old to cuddle," she says, handing Kyle his slushie. "I mean, my parents still do, and they're, like, *old*."

Kyle raises his slushie to her in a salute before he leads Aidan down the hall to their theater. It's empty enough that they can sit in the first row after the stairs. As soon as Kyle sits, he props his feet up on the railing.

"I'm not cuddling you in a movie theater," he warns Aidan.

"Does that mean we're, like, *really* old?"

Kyle laughs and knocks his shoulder against Aidan's before taking a sip of his slushie. If he leaves his shoulder leaning against Aidan's then that's nobody's business.

THE MOVIE IS exactly what it was billed as—low on plot and high on explosives. Kyle emerges from the theaters and blinks against the bright light of the outdoors. He also feels as if someone stuffed cotton in his ears, everything quiet compared to how damn loud the movie was.

He rubs his ear for the third time and catches Aidan staring at him.

Is Aidan about to ask him why hand-holding is okay in public theaters and cuddling isn't?

A couple of scenes into the movie, Kyle put his hand on Aidan's thigh, palm up, and held his breath. He didn't breathe again until Aidan's fingers, greasy with butter, laced with his.

By holding hands, Kyle learned how Aidan has zero sense of foreshadowing. He squeezed Kyle's hand every time something caught him off guard. It was cute, especially when he tried to pull away the first time, embarrassed. Kyle only held on to him tighter and tried not to laugh too loudly whenever Aidan was surprised by the formulaic plot.

They're still holding hands when they reach Aidan's car. Aidan walks Kyle to the passenger side which is both ridiculous and a little bit sweet. Kyle's about to say so when Aidan crowds him up against the car and drags a finger across Kyle's lips.

"How'd they even get this red? You used a straw."

Kyle laughs, unable to help himself.

Aidan's pouting because Kyle's slushie turned his lips red?

"It's a good thing it was dark in the theater," Aidan says. "I wouldn't have been able to keep my mouth off yours if I saw you looking like this."

Like what? He wants to ask but knows the movie theater parking lot is an equally bad place to kiss each other.

"You want to go home?" Kyle asks.

"We have plans," Aidan reminds him. "Walk then dinner."

"Then you'll kiss me?"

There's a beat of awkward silence before Aidan says, "If you want me to," as if he's still unsure where they are.

"I do," Kyle promises. He's feeling better than he was this morning, and while they're far from perfect, they're making strides toward being right again. He wouldn't mind an evening of lazy kisses on the couch. "I want everything we've been doing, and I want to try out the things on our to-do list. I'm not going anywhere." *Not unless you make me.*

"Good," Aidan says. "I mean, me too."

Kyle smiles and drops a brief, chaste kiss against the corner of Aidan's mouth. "We should take our walk. My legs are restless from all the time sitting."

Aidan drives them to the same park they took their first walk together in, back when they'd only just met. They'd set up coffee then, not liking how crowded the shop was, they'd taken their coffees and gone looking for some privacy.

Kyle smiles as Aidan pulls into a parking spot. He doesn't hide it when Aidan looks over at him.

They walk side by side, shoulders brushing with every step. They don't hold hands, because Kyle's too busy using his to recreate some of his favorite explosions and fight scenes from the movie. Aidan watches his recap with a smile and laughs whenever Kyle tries to pull him in.

WHEN THEY RETURN to Aidan's house, they can smell dinner from the moment they walk through the door.

They eat quickly, their feet tangled together underneath the table, because after dinner there's only one thing left on the agenda for the day.

This morning, Kyle wasn't interested in kissing or even holding hands, but a lot has changed since this morning. He wants Aidan's hands in his hair and Aidan's mouth against his, proof that they'll be all right.

As soon as they've washed their bowls and the rest of the soup has been put in Tupperware, Kyle leans against the counter.

"You promised me kissing."

"I did. You want it in the kitchen, surrounded by the evidence of your culinary mastery?"

"Shut up and kiss me."

Aidan's laughing as he steps into Kyle's space and kisses him. He tastes a little like salsa and a little like Oreos, which is a weird mixture, but it doesn't make Kyle break the kiss. It's been too long since Kyle's been able to do this and there were points today where he thought he'd never be able to do it again.

They move into the living room, because Kyle doesn't like how the island counter digs into his back. He pushes Aidan down on the couch then climbs into his lap, pinning him in place with his thighs.

It feels good to have Aidan beneath him and even better when Aidan grips Kyle's hips like he wants Kyle here as much as Kyle wants to be here. It makes Kyle kiss him harder, biting at Aidan's lips then groaning when Aidan returns the favor.

When they pull back to breathe, Kyle drags his tongue over his bottom lip. It's puffy and warm, as if all the blood in his face has rushed to his mouth. Aidan tips them over, covers Kyle's body with his, and kisses him again.

It's a desperate kiss now, Aidan changing things before Kyle can catch up—biting then sucking then thrusting his tongue into Kyle's mouth. It always comes back to Aidan's teeth, sharp against Kyle's bottom lip.

Kyle starts to pull away a couple times so Aidan will chase his mouth and kiss him even harder.

They're both breathing hard when Aidan props himself up on his elbows, ending their kiss. Aidan's cheeks are flushed, and his eyes are bright as he stares down at Kyle. His fingers touch Kyle's lips like they had outside the movie theater and—

"Are you jealous of a *slushie*?" Kyle demands, pieces clicking together.

Aidan's cheeks turn redder.

"You are. You're jealous of a slushie."

Aidan traces the curve of Kyle's lips again with his fingers.

The next time he kisses Kyle, it's softer. He slides his hands up Kyle's side then slips them around his back to hold him closer. Kyle spreads his legs so Aidan will fall between them then hooks his ankles around Aidan's back. Neither of them are going anywhere.

It's sweet and almost too much, but it's exactly what they need.

Then Kyle turns his head away, laughing, because—

"*Slushie*," he says.

Aidan tucks his head against Kyle's neck and laughs too.

Now, they're both laughing and there's no kissing, but Kyle doesn't mind.

They'll have plenty of time for it later.

Chapter Fourteen

KYLE BELIEVES THAT special occasions should be marked with candles. Occasions like going condom-less for the first time should be celebrated with candles, wine, then being fucked until there's come dripping out of his ass.

He scatters a few candles around the apartment, unlit until they're ready for them, dithers over which wine he wants to serve with dinner, then fusses over his apartment while he waits for Aidan to show up.

Kyle's been buzzing all day, anticipation and excitement distracting him from his work. He's not sure he's sat still for more than thirty minutes at a time today.

Will Aidan show up as desperate as Kyle is and shove him against the wall and fuck him there? It doesn't leave time for candles, but they can always do that afterwards. There's definitely an appeal to Aidan wanting Kyle so badly he can't wait to even reach the bedroom. Kyle has a bottle of lube stashed in the entry closet, just in case.

He didn't want to prep himself ahead of time because the couple of minutes it takes Aidan to do that would be the best kind of tease.

Or maybe Aidan will take Kyle to bed and be gentle. In bed, they'd fuck face to face so they were looking at each other the whole time. Maybe Aidan would let Kyle touch him, maybe he'd pin Kyle's wrists above them. When they were done, though, Kyle would have tears on his cheeks and come on his belly and between his thighs, and it would be near fucking perfect.

Kyle checks on dinner, a lasagna they can eat as soon as Aidan arrives or that he can cover with foil and stick in the fridge for later.

He wants to make sure he's prepared for anything.

Aidan knocks.

"Come in!" Kyle calls as he takes dinner out of the oven. He sets it on the cooling racks and turns to see Aidan leaning against the counter.

He looks comfortable, like this is where he belongs, and Kyle shakes off his oven mitts so he can grab Aidan and pulls him in for a kiss.

It's Kyle who pushes Aidan up against the wall, careful of the picture he has hanging there. He kisses him, too aggressive for a *welcome home* kiss, but not aggressive enough to be the start of something.

He's not sure what he'd be starting. He knows the general plan for the night, but he left the specifics up to Aidan.

Kyle has to kiss him again, little stinging bites he leaves against Aidan's lips then the curve of his jaw. Finally, he tucks his head against Aidan's neck and pants. He wants everything. It's overwhelming. He needs Aidan to tell him what they're doing.

"Well," Aidan says, gratifyingly out of breath. "That's a hell of a greeting."

Kyle picks his head up to grin. "Hi."

Aidan laughs. "Hi," he parrots back.

He glances down at Kyle's hands. His fingers are hooked through Aidan's belt loops, holding him close even though Aidan hasn't shown any sign of leaving. Aidan traces Kyle's fingers, moving up over his knuckles, then across the backs of his hands until he's touching Kyle's cuffs.

Kyle prefers Aidan to put them on. He's always gentle, holding Kyle's hands as if they're something precious. Today, Kyle buckled his cuffs himself, because he wanted Aidan to know, the moment he stepped through the door, that Kyle is his.

Anything Aidan wants, Kyle will give him.

"How ready?" Aidan asks. He still hasn't looked away from Kyle's wrists.

"Not that," Kyle says. "I figured you'd text if that's what you wanted."

Aidan smiles as he lifts Kyle's hands so he can press a kiss to the center of one palm then the other. "You figured right."

Heat pools in Kyle's stomach as Aidan flicks his tongue out over his palm. It's—*this* shouldn't be what makes him squirm, but Kyle's breath comes quicker as Aidan kisses up his palm until he can lay the gentlest of kisses right where leather meets skin.

"Oh," Kyle says, then closes his eyes as Aidan does it to his other hand. "Are we?"

"Dinner first," Aidan says.

Kyle nods because he planned for that. He planned for everything, but this is what he hoped for. Even still, need courses through his body, making him antsy, and he'll never make it through dinner like this.

"Kiss me?" Kyle asks. "Please?" The way his eyes sweep downward, deferential, isn't an act. He needs Aidan to settle him, to promise that there's something good in his future if he can be patient a little longer.

Aidan doesn't tease. He reels Kyle in and kisses him, different from the kiss Kyle greeted him with. It's less desperate, Aidan's lips firm and sure, and promises Kyle there will be more of this later.

Kyle presses Aidan against the wall again, but this time he does it because he needs to be as close as he can.

Aidan keeps one hand curled around Kyle's wrist. The other he slides up Kyle's shirt until he can pull Kyle closer.

It's good until Aidan drops his hand away. Kyle breaks their kiss, a protest on the tip of his tongue when Aidan says, "Dinner."

Kyle nods.

Neither of them moves.

Finally, Aidan nudges Kyle's hip. "Dinner, then I'll show you my plan for the night."

That's enough motivation for Kyle to move. Kyle steps back, then turns so he isn't tempted to step into Aidan's arms again. He checks the lasagna to make sure it's still warm, turns the oven back on for the garlic bread, then opens the fridge to grab what he needs for the salad.

"The bread will take a couple minutes," Kyle says. "I didn't want to risk burning it."

Aidan grins as he leans against the counter, looking pleased with himself. He also looks comfortable, at home here in Kyle's kitchen. It brings a smile to Kyle's face, and he ducks his head to hide it.

"Did you think I wouldn't be able to resist you when I came through the door?" Aidan asks.

"It was fifty-fifty."

"I was tempted but—" Aidan's distracted by the kitchen table. "Are those candles?"

Kyle shrugs as he slides the garlic bread into the oven. "Tonight's a big step."

"And big steps are marked by candles?"

"Yes."

Aidan looks at the candles then at Kyle then back at the candles. "Do you want me to light them?"

"Sure. Matches are in the odds-and-ends drawer. Will you grab the corkscrew while you're in there? You can open the wine."

Aidan finds the odds-and-ends drawer right away. He lights the first candle before he says, "Aren't I the one who's supposed to be romancing *you*?"

"You're doing whatever you want with me," Kyle says, and Aidan almost forgets to light the second candle. "After dinner is for your plans. Dinner is for mine. And that means wine and candles."

They sit across from each other for dinner. Kyle's the one who stretches out first, but Aidan's the one to tangle their legs together. They talk about Aidan's classes and Kyle's projects while they eat. The food is good, the wine is better, and halfway through, Aidan reaches his hand across the table. They spend the second half of dinner holding hands, Kyle's candles burning between them.

The whole thing—holding hands, flickering candles, a nice-ish bottle of wine—is probably sappy, but Kyle likes sappy. He also, by the end of dinner, has reached his threshold for sappy. He doesn't want something soft or sweet or romantic tonight.

He's not sure how rough he wants things to get, but he definitely wants to end the night feeling *owned*. He doesn't bother to hide his shiver or his want as he finishes his wine. Aidan watches him with knowing eyes.

Kyle licks his lips then pulls his bottom lip between his teeth. He knows Aidan doesn't like it, because he wants all the marks on Kyle to be his own. Maybe Kyle wants to dare him to get started.

"Don't." Aidan squeezes Kyle's hand tight, a warning. "Don't push me. I have a plan, remember?"

"Sorry."

Aidan squeezes Kyle's hand again, gentler this time. "You're impatient, and I'll give you what you want. But don't make me punish you tonight."

"Okay." Kyle looks at their plates, empty save for some lingering salad dressing and pasta sauce. "Time to clean up?"

"I'll do the dishes while you take care of the leftovers."

It takes them twice as long as it should to clean up, because Aidan takes every excuse he can to touch Kyle. He bumps into him while making trips to the table. He puts two hands on Kyle's hips to hold him still while Aidan leans around him to blow out the candles. He'll touch Kyle's cheek when they're close enough.

Once the plates are soaking in the sink, Aidan even reels Kyle in for a kiss.

It leaves Kyle dizzy with want. When he finishes his part of the cleanup, he leans against the table and watches Aidan's muscles flex beneath his shirt as he scrubs a stubborn bit of sauce off one of the plates.

"I can feel you staring," Aidan says, amused.

"I have a good view." Kyle's gaze drifts down. Aidan's shirt is bunched from where it came untucked earlier against the door. His ass is nicely rounded, even if his pants do nothing for him. "I really need to take you shopping."

Aidan flicks soapy water at him in response. Kyle laughs as he wipes the suds off his cheek. It's Aidan's turn to stare, the teasing glint in his eye replaced with something hungrier.

Kyle opens his posture in response, inviting Aidan to do whatever he wants.

"Find a cushion you like and bring it to the couch."

"The couch?" Kyle asks as he hunts down his favorite cushion to kneel on. It's flat enough that he feels balanced while he's on it and cushioned enough that he can stay down for a while. "I don't deserve a bed?"

"Maybe you can earn it," Aidan says, offhand, careless, even though Kyle knows he isn't.

It makes something hot twist in Kyle's stomach.

He's already half-hard from anticipation alone. He wants to cup his dick while he thinks about all the ways Aidan could make him earn it, but when he looks down, he eyes the catch on his cuffs.

Aidan didn't say he could touch, which means he isn't allowed.

He tightens his grip on the couch so he isn't tempted to touch himself.

"Good," Aidan says.

Kyle's head jerks up. He hadn't realized Aidan was watching him. The other man's leaning against the island now, his arms crossed over his chest, and he's definitely watching.

Kyle flushes, a mixture of Aidan's attention and the praise.

"Put your cushion on the floor, then you can touch yourself, but only through your pants."

He drops his cushion in front of the couch, then presses the heel of his palm against his dick, fast enough that Aidan laughs. Kyle closes his eyes so the sound can wash over him, cheeks flushing and cock twitching.

He's able to stroke himself twice before Aidan says, "That's enough."

Kyle drops his hands to his sides.

"Good," Aidan praises. "Kneel."

Kyle kneels, disappointed when it means the couch blocks his view of Aidan.

He rests his hands on his thighs and bows his head so he can stare at his cuffs. The black leather is almost too stark against his skin. He's thought about buying new cuffs, brown ones maybe, so they'd look more natural against his skin. He hasn't, because these are still in good condition, and it seems like a waste to buy new ones.

Still, maybe it's time.

"Well, aren't you a pretty picture?"

Aidan's voice is close, and Kyle wants to look up and see how close, but he stays where he is. He doesn't want to ruin the picture. He wants Aidan to keep looking. He wants Aidan to *touch*.

There's movement in Kyle's peripheral vision. He can see Aidan's bare legs, the dusting of hair on his thighs. He wants to lift his gaze, see if Aidan's completely naked.

"Arms above your head," Aidan says.

Kyle obediently lifts his arms, and Aidan pulls his shirt over his head, tossing it somewhere behind him.

"Better," Aidan says. "Put your hands back on your thighs, but you can look at me."

Aidan lost his pants and his boxers somewhere, but he's still in his dress shirt. It hangs down low enough to cover his cock, and Kyle glares at the fabric. He wants Aidan completely naked. He wants to see if he's hard yet.

Kyle has a good idea where tonight's headed now; he's on his knees, Aidan's cock is *right there*. He sways forward, but he's stopped by two fingers on his forehead.

"Do you want it?" Aidan asks. He lifts his shirt so Kyle can see the hard curve of his cock.

Kyle licks his lips then nods.

"Words. I want to hear you."

"Please," Kyle says. "I want your cock in my mouth. I want to feel you get all hard. Let me feel how much you want me."

Aidan uncaps the small bottle of lube he brought with him, the one Kyle hadn't noticed because there were so many other things claiming his attention. He drizzles lube on his cock, enough that it doesn't chafe as he strokes himself. "Tell me more."

If Kyle does a good enough job, will Aidan give him what he wants?

"Please," Kyle says again, and Aidan groans. "Let me get my mouth on you. I want to taste you. Fuck my mouth, come in me so I can taste it. We haven't done it before, and I want it. I've been patient. I've *waited*. Please don't make me wait more."

Aidan strokes himself faster, precome welling at the tip of his cock.

Kyle's erection presses hard against his fly. He spreads his knees to try to get a bit of relief. "I'll be so good for you. I'd keep my hands on my thighs, if that's what you want. I'd only use my mouth—wet and messy and a little sloppy until you understand how much I want this. Maybe you'd slide your hands into my hair and make me take it. You'd only pull back long enough to hear me beg for more."

Aidan swipes his finger through his precome and holds it out. It's all the invitation Kyle needs, lunging forward until he can wrap his lips around Aidan's finger. It's good, but it isn't enough, and when Aidan pulls back, Kyle can't help his groan.

He still says, "Thank you," because Aidan didn't have to give him anything.

It's Aidan's turn to groan as his cock jerks in his grasp. He raises his eyes toward his ceiling. Kyle knows all his signs now. He knows Aidan's close. Even if Aidan won't let Kyle suck him, he still wants to see him come.

"Look at me," Kyle begs. "I want you looking at me when you come. Please. Look at how desperate you've made me with barely even touching me."

Aidan does look, his cheeks flushed and his eyes bright. He slides a hand through Kyle's hair, gripping hard.

"Please," Kyle asks, one last time.

Aidan tips Kyle's head back. "Close your eyes."

It's unfair that he won't be able to feel or see Aidan's orgasm, but he closes his eyes. If Aidan wants to jerk off to Kyle's lips, parted and begging for him, or even to Kyle's obedience, then he can. Kyle will kneel here and give him exactly what he asks for.

When Aidan comes, it's with a breathy gasp, and Kyle's caught off-guard when Aidan's come splatters across his face. He barely remembers to keep his eyes closed as come lands across his eyelids and cheeks. The best is the bit that lands on his lips. Or maybe it's the worst, because Kyle wants to run his tongue over it and swallow, but Aidan hasn't told him he can move.

So Kyle stays, fingers digging into his thighs, eyes closed and body trembling, as he waits to be told what to do.

Aidan drags his thumb across Kyle's bottom lip. Kyle whimpers, afraid he'll be denied this too, before Aidan pushes his thumb into his mouth.

"Suck."

Kyle does eagerly. Will Aidan do this with every bit of come he left on Kyle's skin? He shifts from knee to knee, *hoping*. Aidan's had his release, but Kyle's still hard in his pants, desperate for any kind of touch Aidan will give him.

"Here's the deal," Aidan says, drawing his thumb from Kyle's mouth. "I'm going to rub my come into your skin."

Kyle doesn't try to hide his shudder.

"If you can get yourself off before I'm done, then you're allowed to come. As soon as I'm done touching your face, you're done touching your cock. Understand?"

Kyle nods, a vigorous shake of his head. "May I open my pants?"

"How else were you planning to get off?" Aidan laughs, a little mean, and Kyle has to press his hand against the front of his pants as his dick jerks at the sound. They'll have to revisit Kyle's idea for the light humiliation scene. Aidan hits the perfect chord, condescending and hot, and that's when they haven't even planned it.

Kyle unbuttons his pants then shoves them and his briefs down as far as he can while he's still on his knees. He wraps a hand around his dick and wonders if he should ask for the lube. Would Aidan toss it to him like he didn't care? Would he toss it away and say, "Too bad"?

He has to squeeze his cock, because if he doesn't then this will be over too soon. It feels good so he squeezes himself again. It defeats the purpose of what he's trying to do so he tugs on his balls, hard enough to clear his head and chase away the worst of the danger. There's so much going on, all of it good, and he doesn't want it to be over. He wants to kneel at Aidan's feet for as long as Aidan will let him. He wants to touch himself and be touched and—

"The point is for you to get off," Aidan says. His fingers trace Kyle's lips.

"I will." There's no way he won't. The right touch, maybe even the wrong touch soon, and he'll come all over his fist. But first, "You said you'd rub it in. Please?"

Eyes still closed, all Kyle can do is tilt his face up and hope Aidan keeps his promise.

He begins with Kyle's cheeks, where tears and come mingle. He rubs in slow circles, the kind of rhythm that could put him to sleep if what Aidan was doing wasn't so filthily hot. He keeps his strokes light, a background to the main show. He's aware of his orgasm building, but it's like a low simmer; there, on the edge of something more but not quite.

Aidan sweeps his thumbs across Kyle's cheeks. They're gentle on his eyelids, then rougher against his forehead. He covers every inch of Kyle's face until he warns, "Last bit."

Kyle gives himself permission to come, cock spurting in his hand as Aidan rubs the last of his release into Kyle's skin. Kyle wipes his hand on his stomach, then sinks down onto his knees. He doesn't open his eyes so he can cling to this feeling.

He feels...perfect. He's marked and *claimed*. The only thing that can make tonight better is if they cuddle in bed, trading lazy kisses until they both fall asleep.

Kyle opens his eyes. Does he look as dazed as he feels?

Aidan catches Kyle's face between his hands. "Incredible," he murmurs before bending down to kiss him.

They kiss until Aidan's back must hurt then Aidan pulls back. "Shower, then bed."

"I've earned the bed, then?" Kyle asks as Aidan helps him to his feet.

Kyle's pants and briefs are at his thighs. He doesn't want to pull them back up or waddle around the apartment in them. He shoves them down to his ankles, then steps out of them.

"Definitely," Aidan answers.

Kyle grins as he sways closer. "How optional is the shower?"

Aidan looks pointedly at the come drying on Kyle's stomach. "Not optional."

Kyle laughs and laces his fingers through Aidan's. "All right, shower, then you're cuddling me."

"You're the one who does the octopus impression in bed."

"I have to make sure you aren't getting away."

Aidan stops in the middle of the hallway. His free hand circles the cuff on Kyle's wrist. "I'm not going anywhere. Not unless you want me to."

There's nothing for Kyle to do but kiss him.

It takes them a long time to reach the shower.

Chapter Fifteen

WEDNESDAY NIGHT FINDS them at Enchanting Encounters, because Kyle's just wrapped up a big project, and he wants a celebratory beer. Wednesday nights aren't very popular, which means they find seats at the bar with ease.

"You're out partying on a school night?" TJ asks as he sets a beer down in front of each of them. He tsks his tongue. "Aren't you supposed to be a good role model?"

"I have afternoon classes tomorrow," Aidan answers, as if he wants to make sure TJ knows he's responsible.

It's cute, and Kyle slides his stool closer so he can rest his hand on Aidan's thigh. He's tempted to slide his hand higher, but they came here to relax and have a nice evening out. They're not here to start anything.

"So, what's your excuse, then?" TJ asks Kyle.

Kyle grins. "I finished a project and sent out two invoices. I used up all my responsible, so we're celebrating."

"Oh, yes," Aidan agrees. "You and your two beers are getting wild."

Kyle laughs and leans into him. His smile grows when, instead of pushing him off, Aidan wraps an arm around Kyle's shoulders to keep him tucked against his side.

"You two are sickeningly cute," TJ says. "Let me know when you want your second beers."

"Thanks."

Kyle stays close to Aidan while he sips his beer. They probably could've done this at one of their places; cracked open a few beers and sat on the couch while they watched TV or maybe with some music playing, but Kyle's glad they went out. With each passing day, Kyle grows more certain that Aidan's the only person he wants to have sex with for the rest of his life, but he's not the only person Kyle wants to talk to for that time.

Kyle's a social guy, and as much as he loves being shut away at one of their places together, getting out and seeing other people is good too.

"Do you want something?" Aidan asks.

Kyle lifts his head off Aidan's shoulder to hold up his beer. "It's still mostly full. And I already have you."

Aidan's eyes are soft around the corners as he leans in to press a kiss to Kyle's lips. "Something special, I mean. For a project well done."

Aidan wraps his fingers, loose, around Kyle's wrist where his cuffs would be if they were scening. Kyle's gaze is drawn to where they're touching, and he can think of at least a dozen things he wants to do, but he shakes his head.

"This—" he holds up his beer "—is how we're celebrating a project well done. We can bring my cuffs out later because we want to. I don't want to mix the two things up."

"Sounds good."

"But you can keep holding me like this. I like it."

Aidan smiles and tightens his grip just a little bit more.

THEY'RE ON THEIR second beers when Caitlin approaches them, hesitant. "Am I interrupting?" she asks, hovering next to a bar stool but not sitting down.

"Not at all," Kyle answers. "We came out to be social, but you're the first person brave enough to actually talk to us."

"In their defense, you're sending out a strong couple vibe." She sits down in the stool next to them and glances at Aidan. "Is this your, uh—?"

"Partner," Kyle supplies. "And yes. This is Aidan. Aidan, this is Caitlin. I met her during your week of errands."

Kyle still hasn't found out what the surprise is that took Aidan away from him for a whole week. Will he find out before their three months are over? They only have another two weeks left in their extension. It's not enough time for everything Kyle wants.

Aidan sets down his beer so that he can shake Caitlin's hand without having to let go of Kyle. "Nice to meet you."

Caitlin shakes his hand then glances at Kyle. "Um, now that you're here, can I still talk to Kyle or do I only talk to you?"

"You can talk to both of us," Kyle answers. "We're not into the kind of play where everything goes through him. And tonight, we're not playing at all. We're just two guys having a drink at the bar and chatting with a nice woman."

Caitlin's gaze dips to where Aidan's still holding Kyle's wrist.

"Not *just* two guys," Kyle amends. "But we're being boring tonight. How's your search for a man of your own?"

"Okay, I guess? I'm still figuring out what I like, which makes me feel like I should hold off on scening until I do know, but how am I supposed to figure it out unless I try things?"

"That's always tough," Kyle says. "Have you talked to Wanda? I know you filled out the newbie survey, but she's great about setting people up with mentors. There's nothing that says you have to do this on your own."

"A mentor sounds nice. There's so much to learn, and I don't want to make mistakes. Making a mistake here could hurt someone."

"You have good instincts. Pair those with practice and a good teacher and you'll be all set. Do you want a drink? I bet I can get TJ's attention."

"Are you sure?" Aidan asks. "I heard he's the one person in this whole club immune to your charms."

"He's not *immune*. I'll give you resistant, though." Kyle slides into Aidan's lap then turns to grin at him. "To make myself taller."

"Uh huh," Aidan says, but he wraps his arms around Kyle's waist to keep him from going anywhere.

He waves obnoxiously until TJ makes his way over to them.

"I thought two was your limit," the bartender says.

"I'm done after this," Kyle says, "but Caitlin here hasn't even started."

They chat with Caitlin for a bit, then Lou and Jamaal, but they call it an early night. They head home together, Aidan following Kyle up to his apartment.

"Are you staying the night?" Kyle asks as he pours them each a glass of water. "Or did you come up for a cup of coffee and a hand job?"

Aidan laughs as he takes his shoes off. "How are you so sweet and crude at the same time?"

Kyle grins and nudges one of the glasses closer to Aidan. "I don't actually have any coffee."

Aidan laughs harder and ignores his glass of water. He snatches Kyle's out of his hands instead. "I guess I'll have to settle for the hand job."

"There'll be no settling." Kyle takes his glass back and drinks half of it in one go. "How about I tell you something I've been wanting to try, and if you like it, then I'll tell you everything I want you to do to me while I give you that hand job."

"I think that's a yes on staying the night." Aidan takes Kyle's glass from him and finishes his water before he puts the glass in the dishwasher.

He looks completely at home in his socks in Kyle's kitchen, navigating the space as if it's his own. Kyle crowds him against the stainless-steel appliance and kisses him before he says something like, "Stay here every night."

"Bedroom?" Kyle asks when he breaks the kiss.

"It depends on how messy we're getting," Aidan answers, even as he follows Kyle back to his bedroom. "Last time we had sex before bed neither of us wanted to change the sheets."

"Is this your way of asking if I'll lick your come off my hand when we're done?"

Aidan shoves him up against the doorframe, and Kyle laughs before Aidan's kissing all the breath out of him. He kisses hard with a little bit of teeth, and Kyle groans and opens himself up for more.

His lips are stinging by the time Aidan finally pulls back. He's tempted to touch them and see if they're as swollen as they feel. From the way Aidan stares at his mouth, he thinks they are. Maybe Kyle can switch tonight's plans from hand job to blow job. Of course, then he can't talk.

Aidan swats Kyle's ass and says, "Get your cuffs and I'll put them on."

Kyle's quick to move after that, pulling them out of his bedside drawer and holding them out. Aidan doesn't laugh at his eagerness, but he doesn't rush either. He takes his time, buckling each leather strap with care.

"You could do this every day, and I wouldn't grow tired of it," Kyle says.

Aidan smiles and reels him in for a gentle kiss.

When they separate again, Kyle unbuttons his pants and shimmies out of them. He pulls his shirt off, but he keeps his briefs on. Usually, it's Aidan who likes the tease of clothes and Kyle who can't wait to lose them, but tonight he wants to tease himself a little.

He grabs the lube while Aidan strips down, and his hand hovers over a condom. He wouldn't mind being fucked tonight, and Aidan had a good point about not making a mess. But he also wouldn't mind waiting until this weekend.

Aidan slides up behind him, wrapping his arms around Kyle's waist and pressing a kiss to his neck.

"You're thinking pretty hard."

"Thinking about what I want you to do to me." Or maybe what he doesn't want Aidan to do to him. He turns and gives Aidan a push toward the bed.

Aidan grins as he lets himself be moved. He falls back on the bed, then shuffles backward until he's sitting against the headboard, his legs stretched out in front of him.

Kyle tosses him the lube before he straddles Aidan's thighs. He shifts his weight around until he's comfortable but not sitting so heavily on Aidan that he'll put the man's legs to sleep.

"Plans first," Aidan says, holding the lube hostage. "I want to make sure we're all thinking clearly."

"Seeing Caitlin reminded me of something I wanted to try," Kyle says. At Aidan's furrowed brow, he quickly explains. "Not what she's into, that's not really my thing. But when I was thinking about how terrible I'd be trying to walk in heels, it made me wonder if she'd laugh at me being clueless which led me to you."

Aidan still looks confused.

"I want to be bad at something, and I want you to laugh at me for it. It'd be heavier humiliation than we've played with before, but I trust you with it."

Aidan smiles, his expression fond as he rubs his hand over Kyle's hip. Kyle wants to push into the touch, but Aidan said to wait until they're done talking.

"Is this thing you're bad at sex?"

Kyle nods.

"Something specific or sex in general?"

Kyle hadn't gotten this far, but he could get on board with sex in general. He'd be overeager and fumbling because of it while Aidan watched and debated whether to take pity on him or not.

Kyle squirms on Aidan's lap. "The second one."

"Yeah?" Aidan draws Kyle closer. "Do you want to pick me up at a bar? Do you think that if you want my cock badly enough I won't notice that you don't know what you're doing?"

"Yes. Everything's on the table—hand jobs, blow jobs, you fucking me. Any of it. All of it."

"All of it?" Aidan squeezes Kyle's ass. "Ambitious. Do you think you can handle it?"

"If you wanted me to. How do you feel about improvising? I don't want to know all of the details."

"Only if you promise to use your words to check in. I want to make sure this stays good for both of us."

Kyle nods. "I'm also checking yes on sex tears, bruises, and you being a little mean. Do you want to uncheck any of those?"

"Those are all good for me, but I want to do this at the club."

"Friday or Saturday."

"Friday. And I want all of Saturday together. Maybe Sunday too."

"I won't turn down a weekend full of you. Do you want to use names for this?"

Aidan shakes his head. "I don't want you calling me anything that isn't my name."

"Just two strangers meeting in a bar. Does this mean I'm too desperate for your dick to even ask you your name?"

"Sounds like you."

Kyle laughs and shoves Aidan's shoulder. "Are we done planning, then?"

"I can't think of anything else right now."

Kyle glances down at Aidan's cock. "Can I jerk you off now?"

"And there's that desperation." Aidan grins. "Yes, you can make me come now."

Aidan hands the lube over and Kyle slicks himself up before he wraps his hand around Aidan's length.

"Friday night will be good," Kyle says, confident. "It'll be like our first scene together. Do you remember the alleyway? I was going to take a cab home because I couldn't find anyone to fuck me. And then you showed up."

"I fucked you right there against the wall where anyone could walk out and see."

Kyle groans even though he's not the one being touched right now. He speeds his strokes up. "Maybe that can be part two of Friday's scene. You can teach me to be a good enough fuck for your friends."

Aidan rocks his hips up into Kyle's grasp. "Maybe you're not a good enough student. Maybe I'll share you anyways."

Kyle shifts so he's straddling Aidan's thigh, because he needs something to rub against. Aidan's hands, still on Kyle's ass, encourage him to chase his own pleasure, even as he continues to stroke Aidan.

They stop talking, the room filled now with the sounds of their harsh breathing. Aidan's the first to come, squeezing Kyle's ass as he spills over his hand. Kyle drops his hands to Aidan's hip and grinds down, free to selfishly chase his own orgasm.

He's almost there when Aidan says, "Wait."

Kyle's thighs clench around Aidan's, but he doesn't move beyond that.

Aidan runs his hands up Kyle's back then down, soothing. "We can start the lead-up to Friday's scene now."

Kyle drops his head to Aidan's shoulder as he breathes heavily. "Is this where you tell me I'm not allowed to come?"

"Only if you want to."

"Until Friday?"

"Yes, but you can change your mind any time."

"Okay." Kyle takes a deep breath and tries to push down the steady beat of *want-want-want* that pulses under his skin. "How hard are you going to make this?"

Aidan grins as he cups Kyle's erection. "About this hard." He laughs as Kyle groans against his shoulder.

"I know you'll make it worth it, but I'm probably going to hate you for two days."

"I can live with that." Aidan presses a kiss to Kyle's temple. "I need a shower. I have come all over my hip."

"I'll take my shower down the hall. If I shower with you, then I'll be too keyed up to sleep."

"That's fair," Aidan says but he can't keep all the disappointment out of his voice.

Kyle kisses him, a promise he'll hurry so they can be together again, then they part ways to shower.

They meet up again in bed, and Kyle wears both pajama pants and a T-shirt, even though it'll be flimsy protection against whatever Aidan has planned.

"You look so suspicious," Aidan says. He pats the empty half of the bed. "All I want is to sleep. Promise."

True to his word, Aidan doesn't crowd Kyle as soon as he slips into bed. He keeps his distance which is the only way Kyle's able to fall asleep.

They don't wake up in the same positions. Kyle's spooning Aidan, and—a bit embarrassingly—trying to rub off against him. He tells himself it's a normal response, expected even, given that he went to bed half-hard and woke up mostly hard.

If Aidan hadn't been here, then he would've woken up rubbing off against his bed. In comparison, trying to get off with his partner isn't as bad.

As soon as Kyle realizes what he was doing, he rolls away. There's no point in needlessly torturing himself. Maybe he can slip away and sneak a shower before Aidan wakes up.

"I think you had the right idea," Aidan says, his voice thick with sleep.

There goes Kyle's chance to escape.

"I'm pretty sure it was the wrong idea."

Kyle flops onto his back. He's hard enough that he tents his pajama pants. Aidan props himself up on his elbow so he can watch Kyle. A slow smile spreads across his face. *Unfair, no one should look that devious this early.*

The expression softens as Aidan tugs at Kyle's waistband. "Can I?"

This is what you wanted. Last night, you wanted to wait, and you wanted a tease. This is both.

"Yes," Kyle answers.

Aidan pats Kyle's hip. "Pull your pants down to your knees and lie on your stomach."

Kyle obeys, shoving his pants down before he flips over. Morning sex is a good way to wake up. They don't always have the opportunity, because Aidan teaches, but he has late classes today. Good thing too, because they're both too sleepy to make this fast.

"Don't come," Aidan reminds him.

He reaches across Kyle to open the drawer. Kyle spreads his legs as much as he can with his pants still on, but Aidan closes them again.

"All you have to do is stay just like this," Aidan says.

He drizzles lube between Kyle's ass cheeks without bothering to warm it up first. The initial chill is enough of a contrast to Kyle's sleep-heated skin that his erection flags. Then he realizes what Aidan's about to do.

He holds himself as still as he can as Aidan slides his cock between Kyle's cheeks. He drops his forehead to his folded arms and bites back all the sounds that want to escape. It's too much, and not nearly enough. Kyle wants to spread his legs and invite Aidan to fuck him for real. He wants to touch his cock, quick and desperate.

Instead, he squeezes his eyes shut.

"Is this what you were thinking about when you woke up this morning?" Aidan asks. One of his hands is anchored on Kyle's hip while he strokes the other through his hair and down his back. It would be soothing except Kyle's so keyed up even the barest of touches makes him want more.

He grinds his hips into the mattress, because he can't help himself. His cock slides against the sheets, and he's fully hard now, but he knows he won't get off like this. All he's doing is winding himself up even more, but he can't stop.

Aidan's over him, on him, so close to being *in* him, and Kyle thinks he'll explode if he doesn't get some kind of pressure on his aching dick.

By the time Aidan comes all over Kyle's skin, Kyle's one good touch or maybe even the right word away from coming. As soon as he has the space, Kyle pushes up to his knees, cock hanging heavy between his legs.

He breathes hard, hands fisted in the sheets.

"I need a shower," he finally says. "Alone."

Aidan runs a hand through Kyle's hair, messing it up. "Are you still good?"

Kyle pushes his head into Aidan's hand like an overgrown cat. Aidan obligingly pets him.

"I want to come, but I don't need to," Kyle answers.

Aidan leans in to kiss Kyle's cheek. "Take your time in the shower. I'm making breakfast."

"Oh?" Kyle asks, suspicious. That seems like a good reason for him to hurry in the shower.

"I can handle Bisquick and a waffle iron," Aidan promises. "And, if I'm feeling daring, I might even cut up some fruit and put it in yogurt."

"Very daring." It's Kyle's turn to steal a kiss. He twists so he's on his back on the bed, which means he's now gotten Aidan's come on the sheets. He supposes it was time to do laundry anyway.

He tugs Aidan down for another kiss.

Aidan lets himself be moved, but he takes control of the kiss, gentling it every time Kyle grows too desperate. He wants to push for more and more and more, but every time, Aidan draws him back, gives him something different.

"I promised you breakfast," Aidan says when they finally break their kiss. He immediately follows his statement up by dragging his thumb across Kyle's bottom lip.

"Eating is overrated."

Kyle presses a kiss to the tip of Aidan's thumb, but when he tries to suck it into his mouth, Aidan pulls back.

"Breakfast."

Kyle sighs, but Aidan is determined. He climbs out of bed, leaving Kyle no choice but to peel himself off the bedsheet so he can shower.

He wouldn't call his shower pleasant, but by the end of it he doesn't feel like a single touch will set him off. He feels in control of his body again. He pulls on his comfiest pair of sweatpants and a well-worn T-shirt.

After a moment of deliberation, he grabs his cuffs before heading into the kitchen.

There are two plates of eggs and waffles on the island counter, and Aidan's standing next to them, proud. "I decided fruit was too daring, after all."

"It looks good," Kyle says. He catches Aidan staring at his cuffs. "I was thinking I'd wear them today. Will you put them on for me?"

"Yes," Aidan says, gratifyingly quickly. Then, "Is everything still okay?"

"Everything's good, but I like the reminder."

Any time he's tempted to touch himself, he'll see the black leather first, a sign that when he comes isn't up to him right now. He's given that decision over to Aidan. He likes giving control of something so personal to someone else. It's a reminder of how much he trusts Aidan, that he can put his body in Aidan's more than capable hands and know Aidan will take care of him.

Aidan moves into Kyle's space, hands gentle as they buckle his cuffs. "I'd like to come over after work."

"You want to check up on me?" Kyle teases.

"Yes."

Kyle's smile softens. "I'd like that. Can I text you some things to pick up from the store on the way? I'll make dinner, then we can watch the news. It'll be like we're real adults."

"We are real adults, but, yes. Anything you want, all you have to do is ask."

Kyle's pretty sure they aren't talking about groceries anymore.

Chapter Sixteen

BY FRIDAY NIGHT, Kyle's ready to vibrate out of his skin. This isn't his first time playing with orgasm denial, but normally when a Dom tells him not to come for a couple of days, he's left alone to suffer.

Aidan's *everywhere.*

He backed off enough near bedtime that Kyle's able to settle down to sleep but Friday morning, Kyle woke up with Aidan's mouth warm and wet around his cock. He sucked him until Kyle cried then wiped away the tears with gentle fingers.

Kyle's finally at the club which means their scene is only a handful of minutes away. He hopes Aidan isn't looking for any kind of stamina, because Kyle's pretty sure he'll come as soon as he sees Aidan.

He was told to hold out until their scene and that's all he'll be able to manage. He rubs his wrists, bare because they're at the club, and wishes he'd worn his cuffs anyway. When the waiting grew unbearable, he'd cinch them tighter until the leather bit into his skin and he could imagine it was Aidan's fingers holding him that tight. It was the reminder he needed to take a few deep breaths and bring himself back under control.

He wants that reminder back.

They forgo the cuffs at the club because they don't need them to show that they're in a scene. As soon as Kyle steps into the room they're renting, he's acknowledging that they're in a scene. It doesn't stop his wrists from feeling naked without them.

He rubs them again, wishing Aidan was here to curl his fingers around Kyle's skin and press bruises where the cuffs should be.

Soon.

Once inside the room, he loses some of his uneasiness. He smiles as he looks it over, because it's the same setup as their first scene. The door opens into a narrow room designed to look like an alleyway. The walls are painted to resemble brick and there's even a dumpster against the far wall, though, thankfully, it doesn't smell like an actual alleyway.

There's a second door with a neon MOTEL sign above it. The E crackles, light fading in and out.

Fantasy is an amazing thing.

The second room is set up like a motel with a bed along one wall and a couch and a single armchair in front of the TV. Kyle drops his overnight bag near the bed then he goes into the bathroom to splash some water on his face.

When he looks up, he's met with his own reflection. He's in his winter jacket and sweatpants, because there's an inch of snow on the ground, but there's already a flush in his cheeks. His eyes are wide, pupils dilated, and his bottom lip is red from how often he's bitten it today.

He looks halfway fucked already, and Aidan isn't even here.

He's here half an hour early because he wanted to make sure he was ready for Aidan, but that means he needs to get ready.

Aidan painted a nice picture—Kyle desperate to be fucked, but with no clue how to make it happen—and Kyle knows how to dress the part. He was desperate, overeager, and completely out of his depth until he met Wanda and she introduced him to the safe and sane part of hooking up.

He strips down and ignores his cock, which is already beginning to thicken. The jeans he picked for tonight are ones he hasn't worn in five years but found buried in the bottom of his drawer. They were tight the last time he wore them and they're even tighter now. He's pretty sure he hears a few seams pull as he wiggles into them. Zipping them is painful, but he doubts he'll be in them for long.

His black mesh shirt is next. He eyes his makeup kit, debating if eyeliner is pushing it too much. In the end, laziness wins out. He hates falling asleep in eyeliner, but he also hates having to scrub it off when all he wants to do is collapse in bed and sleep.

He does put on a touch of mascara, because it makes his eyelashes look even longer than usual. Then he spends too long trying to make his hair look artfully messy instead of just messy.

The end result is someone who looks like him but isn't quite him. He looks like his younger self, when he thought picking up was about the clothes he wore instead of how he wore them.

He packs his bag again and brings it back to the bedroom. He leaves his pajamas in a neat stack on top.

His phone has no messages. He sends one, *ready when you are ;)* then sets the phone on the nightstand. He won't need it for the rest of the night.

Nerves and anticipation begin to bubble up inside him. His cock presses, hard and painful, against the line of his zipper. Tonight will be good but he doesn't know exactly why. The mystery of the night's plans combined with the past couple of days of need are enough to make his palms sweat.

He wipes them on his jeans then leans against one of the alley walls to wait for Aidan.

He doesn't have to wait long.

As soon as he hears the click of the lock, he slouches against the wall. He spreads his legs as much as his jeans will allow, not much, but enough, because Aidan stops in the doorway and stares. Kyle smirks which isn't quite in line with his planned demure seduction.

"I see subtlety isn't your strength." Aidan steps far enough into the room to push the door shut as if he doesn't want anyone else seeing Kyle like this.

"I got you, didn't I?"

Kyle pulls his bottom lip between his teeth because he knows Aidan doesn't like it. Aidan's still too far away, but maybe he'll close the distance between them, grab Kyle's chin in his hand, and tell him to cut it out. Maybe he'll kiss Kyle, hard and bruising so it's his teeth sharp against Kyle's skin.

Is it too soon to pop the button on his jeans?

"You have my interest," Aidan says, a distance in his voice that Kyle isn't used to. "But can you hold it? What're you offering me?"

"Anything," Kyle says, breathless, and he wishes it was just an act. "I'll make it good for you."

"Hmm." Aidan looks him over again then his eyes flick away, finding him wanting. "Maybe I'll make you good for me."

Kyle sags against the wall, relying on it to hold him up as his knees shake. His heart beats fast and loud, the sound filling his ears. "Please," he says, already imagining the way Aidan would take hold of him then move him wherever he wants him.

"That seems like a lot of work. I'm not sure I want that tonight."

"I won't be. I'm easy, promise."

Kyle flushes as soon as he says it. His flush deepens as Aidan laughs, sharp and cutting.

"Is that so?" He stalks forward, closing the distance between them in a few easy strides. Kyle's already against the wall, but he isn't pinned until Aidan curls his fingers around his hip. Holding him still.

His other hand tilts Kyle's chin up so Aidan can get a good look at him. Aidan's wearing a new cologne, stronger than what he usually wears. It easily wraps around Kyle until all he can smell is something deep and rich and not quite Aidan.

"Oh," Kyle breathes, mouth parting around the word.

Aidan slides two fingers into Kyle's open mouth. They taste faintly like beer as if they really did just come from the bar. Kyle's tongue flutters against Aidan's skin. He wants to suck, wants to look up at Aidan through his lashes and moan, but he's not sure if that's too much too soon.

"You certainly have a mouth for cock," Aidan says, "but I'm not sure you'd know what to do with one once you had it."

Kyle's blush burns its way up to his ears. He wiggles, trying to get the hand on his hip closer to his cock. A minute or two more of this and the sheer force of his erection will bust his pants. He's been hard for so long. If he can only undo the button on his jeans and give himself a little relief.

He reaches his hand down and, in an instant, both his wrists are pinned to the wall on either side of him. One of his wrists is damp from the fingers that had been in his mouth. He tips his head back, exposing his throat, and whines. He's trapped now, no friction on his aching cock.

This is what I wanted earlier. I wanted his hands on my wrists, making sure I know who I belong to.

There's no doubt in Kyle's mind who's in charge.

"Here I thought you were begging for it in the bar," Aidan says, leaning in, his voice low near Kyle's ear. "I didn't realize it was a preview. Are you going to beg me for my cock?"

"Yes." He flexes his wrists so Aidan will hold him tighter. If he had more give in his pants he'd wrap a leg around Aidan's waist and haul him closer. He's so close to what he needs, but Aidan dangles it just out of reach. "Do you—should I start now?"

Aidan's laugh is as low as his voice and a touch mean. "Do you think that's a good idea? Begging for my cock out here where anyone can hear you? Are you worried I won't be enough for you?"

Kyle shakes his head, words as trapped as the rest of him.

"Are you sure? Maybe I should show you what I'm working with, then you can decide if you want someone else to join us."

Aidan slots his thigh between Kyle's legs. He's hard too, but Kyle barely gives any thought to Aidan's size, because he's overwhelmed by the press of Aidan's thigh. It's just where Kyle needs it. He's held off for so long, and Aidan promised once they were in the scene. He hasn't given Kyle permission, but he can't expect him to keep himself together.

Can he?

Kyle grinds down against Aidan's thigh, and it feels unbelievably good. He does it again, wrists straining against the hold on them. He turns his face into his shirt, trying to muffle his cry as he comes.

It's obvious what just happened, Kyle's legs squeezing Aidan's thigh as his body rides out the release it's been waiting far too long for.

Aidan laughs. His hands drop from Kyle's wrists to his hips. "I guess you really are easy."

Kyle's face burns even as his cock twitches. Everything is poised on the edge of too much. Kyle looks away, shame and embarrassment and want a confusing jumble of emotions. Aidan grips Kyle's chin and jerks it up to look at him again.

With his other hand, he roughly palms Kyle's spent cock until Kyle's writhing against the wall. It's definitely too much, but the kind of touch that could be exactly enough. He has to trust Aidan to know where that line is, to push him right up to it but not over it. He bites his lip again, lashes wet with unshed tears.

He's trembling.

"You promised to make tonight good for me," Aidan says. "Are you still interested in that?"

He nods.

Aidan squeezes Kyle's cock hard enough to make him gasp. "Words. I want to hear you say it."

"I'm interested," Kyle says. "I want to make you come too. Please, let me?"

"It's a start." Aidan steps away, abrupt enough that Kyle almost chases him. "We'll work on it. You do a good job begging with your body, but your mouth could use some work."

Kyle bites his lip again and drops his gaze to Aidan's waist.

"Quit that." Aidan's thumb presses hard against Kyle's chin until he stops biting his lip. "I've already said yes to you."

"Okay." They stand in silence long enough that Kyle squirms, comfortable. "Should we go somewhere, then?"

"I know a place."

Aidan leads Kyle through the door to the bedroom with a hand on his hip. Kyle pauses inside the doorway when he sees the large bed. "You, uh, move fast."

Aidan pushes him forward. "This is what you wanted."

Kyle went to the bar planning to flirt until he found someone who was interested in him. He got lucky with this guy. Kyle didn't even have to say anything. He glanced at him a couple of times and wrapped his lips suggestively around his beer. When he left the bar, the guy followed him.

The guy.

Kyle doesn't even know his name. He has his own come cooling in his pants, and he's in a motel room ready to fuck a complete stranger. Shame and arousal tangle in his head again, wires crossing until he's breathing heavily.

"Um," he says, once he's wrestled down the arousal and is left with the shame. "I'm—"

The guy covers Kyle's mouth with his hand. "I don't care what your name is. You introduced yourself by sticking your ass out in the middle of a crowded bar, so I don't think you care much about names either."

Kyle trembles in Aidan's hold.

"When I drop my hand, you're going to strip and show me what I'm working with. Nod if you understand."

Kyle nods.

"Good."

There's enough praise, enough *Aidan* in the word that Kyle feels something in him settle.

Aidan releases him and Kyle stumbles back a step before he pulls his shirt off. He sits on the bed to remove his shoes, afraid of falling over. His socks are next. Then it's time for his pants, and it's a struggle to peel them off. He shimmies as he pulls them down.

"Not a bad show," Aidan says.

Kyle casts his gaze up, searching for more approval than that.

"No underwear. How many bad pornos did you watch before coming up with that one?"

"Easy access?"

"Easy access would be if you were already stretched open."

"I, uh, I'm not." Feeling the weight of Aidan's disappointment, Kyle's quick to add, "Next time I will."

"It'd be a good idea." Aidan kicks off his shoes but leaves the rest of his clothes on. "Maybe even get yourself off while you finger yourself so you don't have a repeat of tonight."

Kyle's blush warms him now that his clothes are in a pile on the floor.

"Or maybe you always have a hair trigger."

"I'm not—I don't—"

"Shh. Move to the center of the bed."

Kyle snaps his mouth shut then scoots to the middle of the bed. He stares at the man approaching him. He's still in all his clothes which makes Kyle feel more naked than he is. It's stupid because he can't be more naked than naked, but he wants to hide under the blankets.

"Will you take your clothes off too?"

"Maybe."

The man's on the bed now too. He's on his knees while Kyle's on his back. Even propped up on his elbows, Kyle feels small as the man looms over him. His cock, which never went fully soft, is stirring again. The urge to cover himself up again grows stronger.

"Can I kiss you?" Kyle asks.

The guy curls a hand around Kyle's neck and leans in. The kiss is rough and demanding, and Kyle would've fallen back against the bed if the man didn't hold him up.

He delivers one last stinging kiss to Kyle's lips before he pulls back. "You haven't done that much before, have you?"

"I have," Kyle snaps, a little indignant.

"Just not very good at it, then?"

Kyle sucks in a breath, but Aidan places a finger against his lips.

"I like you better when you don't talk."

Kyle scowls, angry now. He starts to sit up, but the man stays kneeling over him.

The finger against his lips moves to gently pet Kyle's cheek. "You promised to make tonight good for me. And right now, I want your mouth shut."

Kyle presses his lips into a thin line.

"Good." Aidan strokes Kyle's cheek again. "Of course, I think tonight it'll be more like me making it good for you. Luckily, you seem to like everything. I'm going to touch you now. You can moan and beg, but that's it. Understand?"

Kyle opens his mouth to answer before he remembers what Aidan just said, and nods instead.

The man leans in to kiss him again, and it feels like a reward.

He kisses Kyle until he kisses back then he moves his kisses other places, so Kyle's left open-mouthed and panting. He's definitely growing hard again. It's too soon to be comfortable which is a kind of pleasure in itself.

Kyle reaches down to help himself along, but Aidan growls against his neck then grabs Kyle's wrists. He pins them against the bed, and Kyle's hips hitch up, searching for the friction he needs.

"Please," Kyle says. If only Aidan would let him rub off against his thigh again.

"You *are* new at this."

Kyle's dick twitches, and he looks away.

"There are other places to touch that feel good."

Kyle's smartass answer is cut off with a gasp when Aidan grazes his teeth over Kyle's nipple.

Aidan lifts his head, a smile curving his lips. "You didn't know you were sensitive there? How were you planning on pleasing me when you don't even know what makes *you* feel good?"

"Fuck you." Kyle struggles against Aidan's hold, but the man holds him down with ease. "I know how to make myself feel good. I do it every day."

"I bet you do." Aidan lays an arm around Kyle's chest, holding him down. It frees up his other hand, which he wraps around Kyle's dick. It leaps at the attention, and Aidan laughs. "They're the best two minutes of your day, right?"

Kyle glares.

"I was in the alley with you, remember? Two minutes might actually be a little generous."

Kyle's red-faced and sweaty as he struggles again. Agreeing to let some guy fuck him is different than agreeing to let him fuck *with* him.

"Settle down. If you want to show me how good you are at jerking off, then you can, but then I leave. If you want anything more, then you knock it off with the attitude. You promised me easy."

Kyle doesn't need help. He knows how to get off. He just wanted to do it with another person. *Wasn't it better with him than when I do it by myself? Didn't it feel good when he pinned me against the wall and made me come so fast my head spun? Would it be so bad to let him do it again?*

He slowly relaxes against the bed. "Okay."

"Okay?" Aidan parrots.

"Okay, you can." Kyle glares again.

The guy smiles like he thinks Kyle is cute. "I can what?"

"Whatever you want."

"What if what I want is to teach you how to jerk off properly?"

"Fine."

Aidan's smile grows. "You think you'd sound more excited about getting to touch your dick. Stay put." He pats Kyle's hip then moves so he can fetch the lube from the drawer.

Kyle wants to kick him or sit up or do something to prove he doesn't have to listen, but he's afraid the guy will leave. This isn't at all how he thought tonight would go. He figured there'd be some kissing, maybe hand jobs. If he was lucky, then he'd be able to suck someone's dick.

This is different than that. He likes it. And doesn't like it. His face feels too hot, and he wants to turn away from the man's piercing stare and casual dismissal. His dick's completely hard. It leaves his head a jumbled mess, unsure of how he's supposed to feel.

"You still with me?" the guy asks.

Kyle nods.

The guy holds out the lube. "Here's your chance to show me how good you are."

Kyle takes the bottle, hesitant, because there has to be some kind of catch.

"You have to listen, no matter what I tell you. If I say slow down, you slow down. If I tell you to stop, you stop. Got it?"

Kyle nods, then feels the need to say, "This is the weirdest hookup ever."

"Do you want to stop?" The guy tilts Kyle's chin up so they're looking at each other. Kyle thinks he sees a bit of Aidan in his eyes. He definitely heard Aidan in the question.

He's checking in to make sure Kyle's still on board, that his hesitance is all his character and not himself.

"I don't want to stop. I—" The blush that rises in his cheeks is all Kyle. "I like it."

The guy smiles, the friendliest he's looked all night.

"Slick up," he says. "Then touch yourself."

Kyle wraps his hand around his dick. As soon as he does, the guy rubs circles around Kyle's nipples until they grow stiff. He squeezes his dick and arches his back, pushing his chest into the man's hands.

"You used your mouth before."

"It's easier to keep an eye on you this way."

"I liked your teeth."

The man's smile is sharp as he says, "You like it when it hurts?"

He pinches, sudden enough that Kyle gasps, the air punched out of him. It's a sharp kind of pain, his chest now burning as hot as his face. He frantically strokes himself as the stinging pain mixes with the steady pleasure.

"Slower," the man chides. "This is a good opportunity to work on your control."

"No," Kyle says, even as he listens. His hand slows to a glacial pace, the kind that will build him up but won't be enough.

Will this be like the past two days? He's not sure he can handle Aidan winding him up then refusing to let him come. He held out for the scene but now they're here and—

"No?" Aidan asks. He slides his hands down to Kyle's ribs, fingers spreading to touch as much of him as possible. It's a less distracting touch than before.

"You'll let me come before we're done?" The neediness in his voice isn't faked.

"Yes," Aidan promises. There's no mocking lilt to the word, no smile tugging at his lips.

They're both out of character right now.

"We can," Kyle says. If there's an end time to his wait, if there's a goal for him to hold out for, then he can do it.

Aidan kisses him, still out of character, but Kyle thinks both of them need it. He tips his head back to deepen the kiss. He tangles his free hand in Aidan's hair to pull him closer. He doesn't know how long it takes for the kiss to grow less desperate, but as soon as Kyle relaxes against the bed again, Aidan pulls back.

He slides his hands up and digs his nails into Kyle's nipples.

The scene's back on.

He does his best to stroke himself slowly. It's hard when his entire body feels like a livewire, buzzing and crackling. His lips pulse, wanting to be kissed or bitten, but he knows he won't get either of those things. He pushes himself into the man's touch, and his chest hurts as he's played with but hurts even worse when the man pauses. It's the kind of hurt that goes straight to his cock.

He squeezes the base, but that feels good too. His hand speeds up, because he has to. If the guy tells him to stop, then he'll stop.

Only, the man doesn't.

Kyle pants, breath coming quicker and quicker, matching the speed of his hand. He's right on the edge, a stroke or two more, and he'll tip over.

"Stop," the man says.

Kyle can't.

He's too close. He can't pull his hand back so the man does it for him. He grabs Kyle's wrist and pins it to the bed.

Kyle's hips hitch up, searching for the next stroke.

"I guess this was too advanced for you. New plan." He puts Kyle's hands on his chest. "You touch yourself there, and I'll touch you down here."

"Fuck," Kyle groans. He drops his head to his pillow. This means, he won't be coming any time soon.

"Is that something you want?"

Kyle nods.

"Is it something you've done before?"

They didn't cover Kyle's fake backstory before the scene. He nods again, slower this time.

"I guess it doesn't matter if you're lying." Aidan strokes Kyle slower than Kyle ever managed to. His toes curl, his entire body tensing with the need for more. "Either you haven't done it or you haven't done it right."

"You'll do it right?" Kyle asks.

"You won't ever forget this night," Aidan promises.

He drags Kyle to the edge of orgasm, then leaves him there. He pins Kyle to the bed with his hands as Kyle grabs fistfuls of the sheets, because if he touches himself right now he'll come and that's obviously something the man doesn't want. He pushes against the man's hold, not because he's trying to get away but because he needs to move.

Aidan leans more of his weight on him, holding him in place.

There will be bruises on Kyle's hips tomorrow morning, another way for him to remember tonight.

"Can you handle it again?" Aidan asks.

"If you help me."

"Arms above your head. How do your nipples feel?"

"Tingly." He raises his arms and grabs hold of his wrists, because he needs to hold something.

"They'll be sore later. You'll feel it when you put your shirt on."

He grins as if he wants Kyle to have reminders of tonight as much as Kyle does. Kyle returns the smile. Bruises and soreness, a dozen little things that will bring him back to tonight. He wonders what he'll do when those reminders fade. Will he be able to find the man a second time?

"Have you ever touched your balls when you get off?" Aidan asks. He does so now, and grins as Kyle tips his hips up, trying to make Aidan touch him lower. "Ah. This is where you like to touch yourself?" His fingers drag lower. "Have you managed to get even one finger inside yourself before you come?"

Kyle's face flushes, but he's too desperate to summon any kind of real anger. "You'll give me your fingers, right?"

"Yes. And more."

Kyle spreads his legs even more.

Aidan laughs and pats his hip. "Turn over. I want you on your hands and knees."

That sounds promising. He's about to move when Aidan's grip on his hip tightens. "Just a minute."

Kyle sinks back against the bed. He doesn't understand until Aidan returns with a towel.

"To keep you from dripping all over the bed," he explains. "Or I can put a condom on you."

Kyle, cheeks warm with embarrassment, turns over. "Towel is fine." He's pretty sure he'll come the moment Aidan tries to roll a condom on him. He braces his forearms on the bed and lifts his ass. If he wasn't flushed and dizzy with arousal he'd probably be uncomfortable with how exposed he is.

Instead, he shivers when he hears the snap of the lube cap. He drops his head down to rest on the pillow.

Aidan's fingers smear lube around, but not in, his hole.

"Oh, fuck," Kyle says. "You're going to be slow about this too, aren't you?"

"Are you tired of being patient?"

"*Yes.*"

Aidan just laughs and stretches him as leisurely as possible. If Kyle wasn't achingly hard then it'd probably put him to sleep. But all he can think about is how maddening the press of Aidan's fingers is, good but not *enough*. He whines and rolls his hips, only for Aidan's free hand to grip his hip in warning.

"Stay still."

"Please," Kyle begs, fresh tears in his eyes.

By some miracle, Aidan listens. He fucks Kyle with his fingers, relentless, until Kyle's right on the edge again. He doesn't think he can come for this except he's been waiting for what feels like hours.

"Please," he asks again.

"You can," Aidan says. He twists his fingers, and that's all it takes for Kyle to come. Some of it lands on his stomach, the rest on the towel.

He slumps forward and hisses as his nipples rub against the towel.

"You didn't even need anyone touching your cock to come," Aidan says. "First you come in your pants then from two fingers in your ass. You really are easy."

Kyle moans weakly as Aidan's fingers stretch him open. He's too sensitive for it to feel good and too wrung out to try to move away. Aidan rubs a soothing hand between his shoulder blades but even that feels like too much.

"What're you doing?" Kyle asks.

"I haven't come yet," Aidan answers. "And I remember you asking for me to fuck you."

"Oh."

"Oh," Aidan echoes, a little mocking. He pulls his fingers out and wipes them on the towel. Kyle watches him grab a condom from the bedside drawer, then sit against the headboard.

It's a good thing the bed is so big, or they wouldn't be able to fit like this. Still, as Aidan rolls the condom on, Kyle can't believe what he's being asked to do. He's aching, inside and out now. He's exhausted. But it isn't fair to leave the man hanging.

He pushes to his knees and peels the towel off his chest. Come is smeared across both the towel and his skin. He'll need a shower later.

He straddles Aidan and his legs tremble as he lowers himself on the man's cock. He has to drop his head to the man's shoulder and drag in desperate lungfuls of air once he's fully seated. He didn't look big, but now that he's inside Kyle he feels huge.

It feels like every part of Kyle's body has been claimed or marked in some way, outside and inside now. The trembling grows worse. He wants to make this good for Aidan, thank him for everything he's done for Kyle tonight, but he doesn't think he has the energy.

He grinds down and shakes his head as his own cock, soft against his thigh, begins to stir. He doesn't want to get hard again, but he does, slowly and painfully. The more it hurts, the more he squirms on Aidan's cock which makes it hurt more. It's a cycle that he can't break.

He keeps his face tucked against Aidan's neck, and Aidan slides his hand up his thighs then up his stomach.

His fingers brush Kyle's nipples, puffy and sore, and Kyle tries to jerk away.

"It hurts," Kyle says.

"I know. Let it."

Aidan rolls them so Kyle's on his back, his legs hitched up over Aidan's shoulders. It's a different angle, and when Aidan's fingers pinch at Kyle's skin, it makes him clench down on Aidan's cock.

They both groan.

There are tears in Kyle's eyes when he finally comes, cock twitching but nothing coming out. He winces when Aidan pulls out of him.

"You were so good for me," Aidan says. He strips the condom off then strokes himself, as desperate as Kyle had been earlier tonight. He brushes the tears from Kyle's cheeks and comes all over his chest, adding to the mess already there.

Kyle closes his eyes.

Aidan runs his hand through Kyle's hair again, gentle, a different touch than Kyle's been used to tonight. He wants to open his eyes and confirm that it's really Aidan back with him, not whoever Aidan was playing, but that seems like too much effort.

Besides, the kiss Aidan presses against his sweaty forehead is all Aidan.

"I'll be right back," Aidan promises. "I should clean us up."

"Mm."

Aidan laughs quietly, soft and nothing like before. He leaves Kyle's side and Kyle opens his eyes to track his movement. He washes his hands, pulls on a pair of lounge pants, then wets a hand towel.

"I figured a washcloth wouldn't be big enough," Aidan says as he comes back. He wipes Kyle carefully, first the sweat off his forehead then the lube between his thighs then the come off his stomach. He saves Kyle's cock for last and says, "Sorry," before he cleans Kyle there, both as quickly and gently as possible.

It still hurts, and Kyle tries to twist away from the touch. His skin feels raw, and the towel, as soft as it is, scrapes painfully against his skin.

Aidan drops the towel to the floor to join the other. Then he pulls a bottle of water, a bottle of juice, and Jell-O out of the mini-fridge.

"Jell-O?" Kyle asks.

"You need something with sugar, and you don't look up to chewing."

"So, I'm just going to swallow?" Kyle waggles his eyebrows.

Aidan laughs again. He helps Kyle into a sitting position and feeds him Jell-O and holds his water bottle to his lips until Kyle shakes his head.

"Sleep now," Kyle says.

"You'll be hungry in the morning."

"Finishing that cup of Jell-O won't change that." Kyle slides down the bed until he's lying down again. "You can buy me breakfast at the café."

"Okay."

"I was joking."

Aidan settles next to Kyle. "I wasn't."

They'll argue about it in the morning. Right now, Kyle's exhausted. They can't cuddle like they normally do when they sleep together, because right now the sheets are almost too much against Kyle's skin. He can't handle having Aidan touch him. Still, there's something he needs before he can fall asleep.

"Kiss?" he asks.

Aidan shuffles closer until he can press a gentle kiss against Kyle's lips. It's almost too light to be called a kiss. He wants a dozen more like it. He has to turn his head so he won't yawn into Aidan's mouth.

Maybe the kissing will have to wait.

"Goodnight, Kyle," Aidan says.

That—Aidan hadn't called him anything during the scene. They'd been two people—*strangers*—but they aren't anymore.

"Say my name again."

"Kyle."

He kisses Aidan, slow, an end to the night rather than the beginning of one.

"I'm right here," Aidan promises as they separate. "And I'll be here in the morning."

Will you be here for as long as I want you?

Kyle rests his right hand between them, palm up.

They can't spoon, but he does fall asleep holding Aidan's hand.

Chapter Seventeen

HE WAKES UP to an arm slung around his waist and his stomach grumbling. He rolls onto his back and winces as every muscle in his body protests. He's sore, as if he'd gone to the gym for the first time in months. It's the best kind of sore, feeling as if he worked hard the day before.

He slips out from under Aidan's arm so he can use the bathroom. When he pokes his head back into the bedroom, Aidan's still asleep so he takes a shower. The hot water feels amazing. He breathes in steam and stretches under the spray.

He must have lingered longer than he intends, because Aidan's awake when he comes out of the shower, towel slung around his hips. Aidan's sitting up, a worried frown wrinkling his forehead.

Kyle tosses his pajamas on top of his bag. "Morning."

The frown eases, but it doesn't disappear entirely until Aidan holds out a hand and Kyle takes it. Had Aidan thought Kyle left?

He allows Aidan to reel him in then kisses him, a promise that he's here and isn't going anywhere. Last night had been good, different certainly, but good. The whole point of role play is to step into a different persona for a bit. Kyle doesn't think Aidan is who he acted like last night. And, yeah, Kyle had liked playing with that dynamic, but it isn't what he wants all the time.

He wants *Aidan*, just the way he is.

They kiss until Kyle's stomach growls again, loud in the quiet of the room.

Kyle reluctantly pulls back. "Food, then more kissing."

Kyle steps into a pair of sweatpants. When he pulls his shirt over his head, the fabric brushes against his nipples, and he sucks in a breath, because they're still sensitive from last night. Aidan tries, and fails, at not looking smug.

"Yeah, yeah," Kyle says but he's smiling too. "Café? Or somewhere else?"

"Here's good. You can eat again when we're at home."

It's a good point. Kyle doesn't want to wait any longer to eat. The only downside of eating here is that now he wants pancakes, and the café only has basic breakfast foods. Maybe he can have a fruit cup, then drag Aidan somewhere with pancakes that he can smother with fruit and whipped cream.

The café is sparsely populated this early. There will be a larger crowd once people rouse themselves from their rented rooms, and later this afternoon, when it becomes a meeting ground for planning scenes.

Kyle leaves Aidan at a booth with their bags and stares up at the menu. Aidan's breakfast sandwich is easy to order. He's less sure what he wants on his own.

"Egg, definitely," he says. "Bacon. Sausage too. Ham? Is that too much for one sandwich? Actually, I'll take two. One with bacon, one with sausage. And an orange juice. And a fruit cup."

The guy behind the counter grins. "Good night?"

"Very good," Kyle says with a look over his shoulder.

He returns to the table with a tray full of food.

"You're preening," Aidan says.

"Yep. Everyone I see today will know how well you took care of me last night."

His smile grows as he unwraps his first sandwich and takes a bite. The bacon is crispy and the egg is hot and his eyes flutter shut as he chews then swallows. Under the table, Aidan's foot nudges his. There's enough space that it isn't an accident, and Kyle lets their legs tangle together.

Aidan holds his hand on their way to the parking lot. The closeness is something Kyle likes, but he thinks Aidan might need it right now. Last night, Kyle needed to make sure he had his Aidan back. The scene had been good, but the stranger outside the bar isn't who Kyle wanted to fall asleep with. Now that he's awake again, he's good.

It's Aidan who's off-balance, but Kyle's more than willing to stay by his side until he's reoriented. It makes him wish he'd put his cuffs in his bag after all. He knew they were scening at the club, so they wouldn't need them, but they're at Aidan's place now, and he can't quit touching his wrists.

He thinks Aidan could use the extra reassurance of seeing the leather against Kyle's skin.

They're on the couch, shoulder to shoulder, as they watch college football. They're close, but not as close as Kyle expected them to be. He's here to be whatever Aidan needs right now, but he's not sure what that is. Should he drape himself over Aidan? Give him a little space? Kiss him again?

He rubs his wrist again. It would be easier if he didn't have to use his words right now, if he could hold his cuffs out and show Aidan that he trusts him. That he *wants* him.

He shoves his hands in his pockets to keep from fidgeting again.

Aidan draws one of Kyle's hands out of his pockets. He runs his fingers over where Kyle's cuff would rest. "Do you want them?" He rests his fingers against the inside of Kyle's wrist, and Kyle's pulse reaches out to try to touch them with each beat of his heart.

"Not enough to go home and get them."

"Okay."

Aidan turns his attention back to the game, but he doesn't let go of Kyle's wrist. Kyle leans closer, as if Aidan can draw him in with a simple touch.

They watch a few more plays. The purple team has an interception, one of the guys tipping the football then his teammate catching it. Once he's tackled, the game cuts to commercial.

"I'll be right back," Aidan says.

He leaves Kyle alone on the couch. It isn't until he's gone that Kyle wonders if they should talk about last night. Did he push Aidan past his comfort zone? Did he think he couldn't say no? He knows he can be pushy, but he thought they did a good job of communicating and setting boundaries.

He's about to track Aidan down when Aidan returns with a white box in his hands. It's smaller than a shirt box and plain, not even a store logo let alone name on it.

Aidan sits down, a whole half a cushion between them. He holds the box out. "You don't have to," he says.

Don't have to what?

Kyle opens the box. It's full of red tissue paper. He glances up at Aidan, but the man's staring at Kyle's hands. He lifts the first layer of tissue paper. Then the next. At the bottom of the box are two brown leather cuffs.

"Oh," Kyle breathes. He runs his fingers over the smooth leather. "You?" He looks over at Aidan.

"I thought we might want a set to keep at each of our places, so we don't have to worry about bringing your pair wherever we'll be."

Aidan bought him cuffs. He bought him *cuffs*.

Kyle shakes his head. "I don't want mine. These are the only ones I want to wear."

These are a gift. These are something Aidan picked out because he wanted Kyle to have them and thought he would like them. He had to go shopping for them and—

"Was this your secret errand?" Kyle asks. "When I thought you were breaking up with me, were you buying me cuffs?"

Aidan nods.

"We're both idiots." He curls a hand around Aidan's neck and pulls him in for a kiss. It's a brief kiss, because Kyle wants his new cuffs on.

"I had plans for this." Aidan looks down at the box, a little sad. "It was supposed to be special."

Kyle doesn't want Aidan to be unhappy about any part of this. This is the sweetest, most romantic thing anyone has ever done for him in his life. The fact that Aidan did it at all makes it special for Kyle, but if Aidan needs more than that then they can do more.

"Do you have candles?"

"Candles?"

"That's how you make a moment," Kyle answers.

"I don't understand you sometimes." Aidan kisses him as if to reassure him that he still likes him even if he doesn't understand him. "I probably have candles somewhere. They're a common Christmas present from my students."

Aidan leaves the couch again, this time, in search of candles. Kyle stays where he is, box in his lap, staring at his cuffs. They aren't a collar, but they're still a big step. All of Kyle's fears that they'd fizzle out after three months together or Aidan would realize he wanted something different, disappear.

Aidan wouldn't buy cuffs, if he didn't want something more permanent.

Aidan returns with a box of matches and a candle that supposedly smells like a log cabin. He sets the candle on the coffee table before lighting it.

"There," Kyle says. "Mood set."

Aidan eyes the flickering flame. "I'm not sure it's the right kind of candle."

"It's the thought that counts," Kyle says with a grin. Then, because he doesn't want Aidan to think he isn't taking this seriously, he reaches toward Aidan. "The candle isn't the important part."

The cuffs aren't even the important part. Aidan wants to see Kyle in something that's his. He wanted a set of cuffs to keep at his house specifically for Kyle. They're finding more ways to fit into each other's lives, moving closer to each other, rather than further away.

"Does this mean you're interested in another extension?" Kyle asks.

"Yes, but we can save the details for later. Right now, I want this."

Kyle smiles and turns his hands palm up. "Me too."

Aidan cups Kyle's right hand in both of his. He sweeps his thumbs over the smooth skin of Kyle's wrist. He dips his head to brush his lips over the same spot. Kyle's pulse jumps at the first touch, and he can feel Aidan smile against his skin.

When Aidan takes the first cuff out of the box, Kyle doesn't know where to look. The cuff? His wrist? Aidan's face? Aidan is reverent, as if he can't believe Kyle is sitting here with him. He's gentle as he wraps the leather around Kyle's wrist, but he secures it tight enough that when his hands slip away, the press of leather almost feels like being held.

It's a promise, Aidan's touch against his skin even when Aidan isn't touching him. Kyle shakes his head when Aidan reaches for the second cuff. He can't. Not yet.

"Kiss me," Kyle demands, enough desperation in his voice that maybe it's more of a plea.

There's too much feeling in his chest, swelling inside him until he's afraid he'll burst. His hands shake then his shoulders. When Aidan pulls him into his lap, Kyle clings, fingers curling around Aidan's shoulders. He kisses him hard, maybe too hard for the moment they're in, but there's so much he wants to share with Aidan, and no idea how to do it.

He doesn't know how to tell him how addicting it feels to be wanted. He doesn't know how to say how Aidan never treats him like he's fragile but always like he's something precious. He sits, legs on either side of Aidan and Aidan's fingers wrapped around his bare wrist, and tries to show Aidan everything he's feeling.

He would stay here forever if Aidan would let him, held and loved, and it would terrify him if he didn't feel as if Aidan wants him here just as much.

Aidan's the first to break their kiss, resting his forehead against Kyle's as he lifts the second cuff.

Kyle leans back so they can look at each other without going cross-eyed. "If you put that on me, then I'm going deep."

He can already feel the pull, the one that wants to empty him out so Aidan can fill all the space left behind. He'll float, high and far, and the only thing holding him down to Earth will be Aidan's hands on his body and his voice in his ear.

"Do you want that?" Aidan asks.

Kyle holds his wrist out. "Yes."

Then he's falling, falling, falling until Aidan's sure hands catch him and hold him tight.

About the Author

Tamryn studied English and Creative Writing in school but has been writing since she could first hold a pencil. Recently, she's turned her focus toward writing erotica. She enjoys writing stories where sex comes first, then feelings, because doing things out of order can be fun.

Other books by this author

The Daniel and Ryan series
Delayed Gratification
The Start of Something New
Who I Am When I'm With You
Positive Reinforcement
Performance Review
Spa Weekend
Weekend Getaway
Caught in Between
Testing the Limits
Tournament of Champions

The Enchanting Encounters series
To Seek and To Find

Coming Soon from Tamryn Eradani

To Love and to Cherish

Excerpt

MUSIC FILTERS THROUGH the speakers of the dance club, this song less deafening than the last. The singer's voice is lower, crooning, and every beat of the bass reverberates through Kyle's body. He moves with the music, chasing it, his movements too languid to ever completely catch it.

The guy behind him groans as Kyle grinds back against him. He splays his hands across Kyle's hips and pulls Kyle back against him, as if there's any space left between them at this point.

"You're good at this," the guy says, his breath hot against Kyle's ear.

Kyle grins as he tips his head back against the guy's shoulder. It shows off the long line of his throat, even in the dim lighting of the club. It's a tease, all that skin, shiny with a sheen of sweat, more than Kyle meant it to be. The guy tightens his hold as he dips his lips to Kyle's neck.

"Makes me wonder what else you're good at," the guy says.

Yep, definitely too much of a tease. Kyle stops the man's hands from creeping up his shirt.

"Tonight, just dancing," Kyle tells the stranger.

"I could persuade you." He dips his thumbs into Kyle's waistband. It's his turn to grind against Kyle, and Kyle's honest enough to admit that the man's packing a pretty persuasive argument.

It's tempting but he has someone even better waiting for him tonight.

"You can't," Kyle says, apologetic as he turns so they're face-to-face.

The guy's a couple of inches taller than Kyle, but he doesn't make him feel small. He likes a bit of looming from his partners, and he's met some people who pull it off even though they're shorter than him, but this guy doesn't manage it even with a natural advantage. It's a good reminder that while this has been fun, this isn't the guy he wants to spend the rest of his night with.

The man's hands on are Kyle's ass now. They roamed during the past two songs, touching what seems like every part of Kyle's body. His skin is humming with it. He wants a harder touch, for them to slip under his clothes even though he just stopped the man from doing it.

Someone better is waiting for me at home.

Also Available from NineStar Press

Connect with NineStar Press

Website: NineStarPress.com

Facebook: NineStarPress

Facebook Reader Group: NineStarNiche

Twitter: @ninestarpress

Tumblr: NineStarPress

9 781948 608923